Castles of Deferred Dreams

Dorothy Stallworth

iUniverse, Inc.
Bloomington

Castles of Deferred Dreams

iUniverse books may be ordered through booksellers or by contacting:

iUniverse
1663 Liberty Drive
Bloomington, IN 47403
www.iuniverse.com
1-800-Authors (1-800-288-4677)

ISBN: 978-1-4502-7562-0 (sc)
ISBN: 978-1-4502-7563-7 (dj)
ISBN: 978-1-4502-7564-4 (ebook)

Library of Congress Control Number: 2010917398

Printed in the United States of America

iUniverse rev. date: 01/26/2011

CHAPTER ONE

CLEO MARSHALL STRUGGLED THROUGH a night of excruciating dreams. She was swimming underwater in the pitch-blackness of a cavern, desperately fighting off hordes of faceless, nameless, slimy creatures with her bare hands. The water seemed very deep but her feet soon touched cobblestones at its bottom, so slippery that she quickly lost her equilibrium and was pulled downward into the endless depths of the murky waters. Suddenly, she remembered the hidden tunnels and swam skillfully and energetically through them toward a safe haven she knew well, for she had been there many times before. Just as she reached a boat and was paddling toward the open river, she heard a loud gunshot that shattered her into wakefulness and left a lingering scent of gunpowder.

Cleo awakened before dawn, exhausted and despondent. She dressed and, in a fit of panic, drove from the University Guest House, without notifying those who were expecting her at the remaining activities of the Wallace Family Reunion—without saying a word or giving good-bye hugs to the family that raised her.

As she inched her 1941 Buick forward in the early morning fog, a sense of uneasiness hovered over her. The mists surrounding her moved like shrouded sentinels marching recklessly in the car beams' faint light.

A stand of trees confronted her, their wet, leafy limbs swinging with noisy vengeance against her car's windshield, obscuring her view. After a brief struggle, she managed to drive onto a flat surface and realized that she had veered from her intended direction and was instead on the old road to Springhill, Georgia. Not knowing precisely where she was at any given moment had become a familiar experience, as were these disturbing visual images floating before her eyes—several worlds colliding, brightly colored scenes shifting, exploding at last in a silent burst, and the descent of falling stars.

During these brief episodes Cleo fought desperately to hold onto the tale of the "truth fairy" before it fled into the blackness behind the sky. Her doctors called them visual hallucinations—exacerbated by stress, fatigue, and the trauma of her past. Glancing at her watch, she affirmed that only a few seconds had elapsed since the final colorful visions. She considered turning her car around, but some force held her fast to this road and the path she had taken—the road leading to Springhill's center instead of the highway to New Orleans.

After a brief drizzle, the sun appeared again, a ball of fire slicing through a sea of pale blue, its rays veering erratically through the pine forests—the ricocheting flashes of light dancing across the car's windshield. Cleo followed a sudden sharp turn in the road, and in the distance the castle came into view, its turreted main building and smaller dwellings appearing across the distant hills like a child's building blocks, so haphazardly stacked were they against the hazy horizon.

The castle's towers brooded among the clouds like a ghost ship sinking in foamy waters. It seemed grotesquely surreal—an ancient edifice lying astride the shore's ruins after its final decimation. Cleo sat overlooking the dismal scene and wondered what forces had returned her to this place where she had grown up. She had every intention of leaving Springhill for good and never returning. Yet, here she was in this land of her nightmares.

She tried to recall what this place was like before all the trouble, when the castle's buildings and grounds were the pride of the Negro community. She was the first of many orphans who resided at the castle during those years so long ago. She shook her head, remembering how utterly confused she had been during that time. She would never have survived without Cordelia and Albert Wallace, who had managed the castle, and the giant, Isaac Naylor, the wise and learned philosopher who opened his doors to all of them and, in the end, gave his life to save them.

Cleo felt on the verge of tears as a wave of deep exhaustion flowed across her body. She wondered if she would be safe driving to New Orleans now. She decided to find a secluded place to pull off the road and rest. But not here. There were too many people around, and she no longer knew anyone in Springhill. She veered off onto the old road leading to the castle.

She parked her car in a field at the foot of a hill—a hill she had walked up hundreds of times. Fallen limbs, tangled weeds, and thorny vines lay like an impenetrable jungle in front of her. Crumbling walls that looked like ancient ruins surrounded the castle. She rolled down the window and leaned back, gazing through the trees toward the castle up on the hill. She thought she saw smoke rising from its chimneys. "I can't believe it," she said, "someone is living in there." With a blink of her eyes and further scrutiny, she realized that what she thought was smoke were actually wisps of dark clouds floating above the chimneys.

Her thoughts wandered back to yesterday's celebration at Morehouse, where Oscar Wallace, the son of Cordelia and Albert, received a prestigious award for his work among farmers and people of color, having translated their sufferings and successes into several volumes of folklore. She took his book from her satchel: *Climbing Parnassus: Poetry, Folklore, and Music of Southern Negroes*. She turned the pages. There were always references to the castle in Oscar's works, and many people saw the castle as a revered institution. The Wallace family, especially, seemed to believe it deserved an honorable place in history.

Cleo was proud of Oscar, standing tall, so sure of himself and his place in the world. He deserved his awards. Yesterday Oscar had told the story of the castle's history once again, with his customary overly dramatic flair and gestures. What else would one expect of a folklorist? Like a magician, Oscar brought his audience to rapt attention simply by standing before them silently for a few seconds, his piercing eyes roaming the room.

"By embracing the past, you will find your destiny."

He had paused after these words, turned, and looked directly at her. But Oscar had never understood her dilemma. He had good intentions and she loved him, but she could not call upon her devils to reveal themselves at will. They were beyond her control. There were dangers and risks, and she alone would have to face the consequences of opening up those dark, repressed secrets. Heaven only knows how hard she had tried! Even now, even after her so-called "cure," pieces of her inner psyche flew past her as if blown by a fierce wind—too swift to make it whole. She looked around at the tangled, unkempt bushes hung with debris. Along the dangerous path upward lay impenetrable masses of mysterious foliage, covering the landscape of the past. Suddenly, a vision of bloody rivers blocked Cleo's view of the castle. She quickly backed her car out of the brush and drove toward the road, the infernal red dust flying up in clouds behind her.

CHAPTER TWO

ALBERT AND CORDELIA WALLACE, Oscar's parents, had come to Springhill on a mission. The year was 1920, and they were full of hope, passion, and commitment. Quite a few friends and colleagues at Antioch College were shocked when they learned of the Wallaces' decision to leave Ohio for the Deep South. After a number of lavish parties and dinners, peppered with speeches that praised the couple's sense of commitment and moral purpose, they left by train for Springhill, Georgia.

As they walked at last on the streets of the town, they found their clothes too dressy compared to those of others they observed. They were hot and weary, and the red dust clung to the hem of Cordelia's white skirt and white leather shoes.

Albert, who was born about one hundred miles south of Springhill, had been leery of Cordelia's optimistic hopes. The passing of time, however, had cast a soothing light over his pessimistic memories. Even so, he had repeatedly said, "Cordelia, remember we don't have to stay if things don't work out." As he glanced at Cordelia's despairing expression now, he imagined her thoughts of disappointment but refrained from reassuring her.

As they trudged up the steep hill, they were both mortified by the conditions under which Negroes still lived. The shacks opening onto the street attested to their occupants' fragile survival. Many Negroes were walking around barefooted, carrying baskets on their heads, bent over under the weight of sacks of produce.

Albert and Cordelia spoke to each other in choked voices without waiting for answers. "Why didn't someone tell us how extremely backward this place was?" It was as if the ways of the South had been whitewashed out of existence by the pristine snowfalls that blanketed the Ohio winters. They had expected a college town teeming with students, satchels of books over their shoulders, walking with the energetic, determined steps of those who envisioned a better future for their people.

For hours they searched for the address given them in their letter of introduction. However, there was no such address, just a church building where the school should have been. They came upon an elderly Negro woman walking in a slow cadence, struggling under the weight of a basket of groceries.

When they asked her for directions to the high school, she put her burden down and answered in a shrill, hard-edged voice, "You might of passed by the *white* high school way cross town, with all them playing fields round it that runs on out to the river. Now, the *Negro* high school is what you want, and it right here in front of you, Clover Baptist Church. Just go in and go on down to the basement."

Albert and Cordelia were soon looking around the six small rooms in the Clover Baptist Church basement that served as the high school for the entire Negro population of the town. The janitor took them on a tour of the property, explaining that the students used the main church sanctuary as an auditorium for many activities, and that the minister shared his office with the principal. The Wallaces were disheartened to see that the school's books were torn, worn, and outdated hand-me-downs from the white schools.

Miss Wright, a lean woman with an elongated face and bulging eyes who worked as secretary for both the high school and the pastor, appeared at last, saying, "It will be my privilege to take you on a tour of the Springhill Normal School campus in just about fifteen minutes." A normal school offered a two-year course and certification to high-school graduates preparing to be teachers, especially elementary-school teachers. The secretary smiled and sat down at her desk, her interest now focused only on her papers.

Albert was disgruntled and said loudly as they sat on the hard, uncomfortable bench, "I hope the campus classrooms at the two-year normal college are not in the basement of passed-down buildings!"

He glanced at Cordelia, sitting straight and unsmiling beside him, and added, "Maybe, we ... I should have asked for more information before we came."

Cordelia sighed and moved closer to her husband, patting his folded hands and whispering, "Well, I guess we'll just have to make some changes down here we didn't anticipate." She held a church fan to cover her face and added, "Especially after that grand send-off the faculty gave us and the support the Baptist Union expressed in hiring me as your office manager."

Their musings were interrupted by Miss Wright's presence, apologetic and smiling, announcing that she was ready to take them on their tour of Springhill Normal School.

As she drove them through the downtown area, where the whites looked almost as poor and downtrodden as the blacks, Miss Wright asked them to roll up the windows to keep the dust out of the car. Within minutes she turned her car into a driveway bordered by towering pines, behind which they saw the school buildings.

The buildings appeared to have been newly painted—gray, blue, and white. The grounds surrounding the four, three-storied buildings were rife with pine trees, apple trees, crepe myrtles, and magnolias blooming in brilliant colors. The buildings and dormitories were well maintained and clean, and the yards were expertly tended. Indeed the campus seemed like another world from the row of shacks just across the street. At noon they were escorted into the dining room, where a group of home economics students served them iced tea, chicken salad sandwiches, and a dessert of white cake and fresh peach ice cream.

Later that afternoon, Miss Wright took them to their new apartment on the first floor of the girls' dormitory. They were delighted to see the four large, clean, and cheerful rooms with soft, new rugs covering the polished wood floors.

As soon as Miss Wright was out of sight, the couple locked the door, pulled down the shades, and performed together an overly stylized waltz around the rooms to the imaginary strains of *Tales from the Vienna Woods*.

Albert, his arms around Cordelia's lithe body, greedily kissed her lips, cheeks, and neck. They helped each other remove their clothing, while his hands caressed those familiar curves and crevasses of her body that he loved to touch. Still standing, Cordelia wrapped her legs around his muscular torso as he lifted her effortlessly onto him. They clung together, moving in a passionate slow dance, until they fell dizzyingly to the bed and onto the soft blue quilt. They made love until exhaustion overtook them.

Later, they devoured the tea, biscuits, and homemade jam left for them by the Welcoming Committee. At dusk, Albert and Cordelia strolled among the tall pines on the main campus grounds and wandered out onto the tennis courts—only a few hundred yards beyond their apartment—that seemed to be the college's pride. Returning to their home at last, their hearts bursting with love and excitement, they concluded they had not made a mistake coming South, after all.

"Why did you all come all the way from the North to this downtrodden southern town?" This became the most asked question during their first weeks on the job.

Cordelia explained this anomaly to all who asked, "We have decided to use our education and training to uplift members of our race who haven't had the opportunities they deserve. That's why we came here, and that's our dedicated goal."

Albert and Cordelia invited leaders of the community, as well as poor and uneducated people, to teas and receptions. The elite expressed much surprise at these activities, which brought people from different social classes together. It didn't matter whether they came in overalls straight from the fields, or in maid's uniforms, they received the same warm welcome. Many people who had never before entered

Springhill Normal School's grounds were invited to programs, lectures, receptions, and musical recitals. Negroes from nearby communities, as well, volunteered their services. As it was completely segregated, this town had few places for the educated Negro elite to meet; soon they began using the college facilities as their favorite meeting place.

Once in a while, Negro artists traveling in the South gave concerts and stayed overnight as the Wallaces' guests. The venerable Mr. Roland Hayes sang a memorable concert at Springhill Normal shortly after having given a command performance before George V, the king of England. The Wallaces' lives were busy and rewarding, and they made a name for themselves as enlightened leaders in the town. The couple also forged relationships with educators at other colleges such as Spelman and Morris Brown, and even counted as their friends some of the wealthy white benefactors of those institutions. It was at one of their gatherings that they first met the immensely wealthy white southerner, A. C. Treadwell, who would have such a great impact on their lives.

A. C. Treadwell, after amassing a huge fortune from gold prospecting in the West, had returned to his native Georgia with Isaac Naylor, a northern-born Negro and Treadwell's prospecting partner. Treadwell spent several years building an elaborate castle on the northern hills of Springhill, and Isaac Naylor built an adobe house of his own on the vast farmland, in a style that was seldom seen outside the barren regions of the West.

Albert Wallace, as well as being an educator, was a mathematician and inventor. He was hired near the end of Treadwell's castle project to design the electrical, plumbing, and heating systems for the Treadwell castle complex. He never knew how Treadwell learned of his inventions, but when Treadwell arranged a meeting, Albert was amazed that he seemed to already know his entire life's history, his educational achievements, and job resume. And he also had in his possession copies of the patents of most of Albert Wallace's inventions.

Albert seldom saw Treadwell during the building process, but Albert learned early on that money was no object. Anything he needed,

Treadwell would supply—even if he had to order materials from England and France.

Eventually, Albert Wallace's association with Treadwell would make him more financially secure than he ever imagined. Treadwell wrote to his friend, Henry Wilson, with the Department of Agriculture in Washington, recommending that Albert Wallace fill a vacancy as the county agricultural agent. Even though the white county agricultural agent had been in place for many years to advise white farmers, the county had neglected to assign any agent to advise Negro farmers. Treadwell somehow learned that Wallace had graduated at the age of nineteen from the School of Agriculture at Tuskegee Institute and had all the qualifications for the position. He used his prestige and influence to get Wallace hired. The Wallaces were able to move out of the apartment at the Normal School and into a two-story home next door.

Treadwell died in 1924, shortly after his mammoth castle project was completed, giving up his ghost in a retreat high up in the tower of his castle where he most likely looked out—much like an owl from a giant oak—across the vast lands that he owned.

The Treadwell will, drawn up two years before his death and considered a legally unbreakable document, designated that after his death the castle and its immense grounds were to be a refuge and school for female Negro orphans from birth to adulthood. The will indicated that Treadwell's estate was held in securities, as well as gold, precious minerals, and metals all over the globe. His will also left hundreds of acres of land surrounding the castle grounds to Isaac Naylor—the giant—Treadwell's prospecting partner, who was already a wealthy man.

Albert and Cordelia Wallace figured prominently in Treadwell's will. Albert Wallace received a monetary endowment for the development of his own future inventions, and Cordelia Wallace was appointed as the sole trustee responsible for developing the magnificent castle and its considerable lands into an orphanage for females of the Negro race.

People of the Negro middle class rallied their collective energies behind the project and planned innovative programs for the children who were to be the first residents. Albert and Cordelia Wallace promised, "This orphanage will never be like those dismal places you have read about in English novels, and which actually still exist in England and America."

On a fine Sunday morning in May 1924, Cordelia and Albert headed for the castle, driving their car to the opening in the woods. The first part of their journey on foot was daunting, with rutty uphill paths and twisted vines underfoot, but soon they saw ahead of them a graceful arch formed by a column of tall live oak trees that promised shade along their way. Several squirrels chasing acorns scampered near their feet and ran into adjoining green meadows decked with brightly colored wildflowers. Cordelia was leaning heavily on Albert's arm for support when they came at last to level ground where the air was filled with the fragrances of the surrounding camellias, azaleas, jasmine, and hydrangeas in a dazzling array of color. The castle's large, arched oak doors dominated the stone facade; leaded glass windows, parading on either side, glistened gold in the afternoon's sun. Their eyes moved upward, following the tower as it rose majestically toward the sky. As Cordelia and Albert strolled the castle's grounds, delighted with the beauty of the surroundings, they both said in unison, "It's so peaceful here." And Cordelia added, "I feel as if only good things can happen here."

Cordelia continued, almost floating along on air, waxing poetic about the lawns and the gardens, the little bungalows for the staff, and a park where their children, Oscar, six, and Ophelia, four, could play among the flowers, and where families would live together in communion and safety.

Later, they entered the main door of the castle using the large skeletal key, and while Albert headed for an inspection of the heating and electrical systems that he had designed, Cordelia walked through the rooms, delighting in the natural wood wainscoting, the crystal chandeliers, and the tiled fireplaces. After she inspected the large bedrooms and baths, Cordelia called out, her voice echoing in the vast halls, "Albert, I think we should just move in here ourselves!"

Albert came up the stairs and said, "The lighting and heating are in excellent shape. I think you and your board of directors can begin hiring the staff anytime you want. I've made those schedule changes you asked for so Alice King can take over as director while still teaching a course or two at Springhill Normal. And I will be glad to get on with my work with the farmers' union—at last!"

The next few weeks buzzed with activity, as the members of the new staff made exciting plans for the opening of the orphanage. Springhill Normal students volunteered for tasks from setting up beds and adding shelves to sanding tables and cleaning floors. Fragile antique furniture was moved to the vast, dry stone basement and covered with tarpaulins.

Board members and staff provided tours of Hope Memorial, the orphanage's first name, and notices about its opening were placed in churches and businesses. Flyers were tossed in bundles at train and bus stops.

After inviting all the town's Negro ministers for a sumptuous feast on the castle grounds, with music provided by the Springhill Normal Choir, preachers of many denominations sang the praises of the castle as the "promised land" for orphaned Negro girls.

CHAPTER THREE

THE CASTLE'S CLEANING WOMAN heard the knock on the door, a sound so loud that she anticipated the sheriff or some other town official. She searched the area, looking through both sides of the diamond-shaped leaded glass panels, and even though the overhead light cast a fairly strong beam, she saw nothing at first, her vision obscured by the mist of a spring drizzle. Slowly she opened the door, the slice of light from inside casting its lens on a small creature, a blanket partially obscuring a face, the body shaking so violently that the woman reached down, grasped the bundle, and dragged the small figure indoors, holding her tightly as she slammed the door with one foot. She heard the rush of heavy footsteps as someone ran toward the rear of the building, making thud-like sounds in the sod.

If it had not been for the child's physical appearance attesting to her need of immediate medical attention, the cleaning woman—a feisty, strong, and stocky woman—might have followed the footsteps to find that "dastardly person" who would leave a sick, trembling child out in the rain. The child's little body continued its violent thrashing. Her face was contorted with pain, and she was as hot as a lit oven. The little girl's sweaty hands held a brown envelope.

Fortunately, Mrs. Alice King, the head mistress of Hope Memorial, was working later than usual in her office. She immediately called Dr. Cyrus Lee, Springhill's only colored physician. By the time he arrived twenty minutes later, the little girl was lying on a clean bed on the sleeping porch.

Dr. Cyrus Lee was an elderly light-skinned man, with a large brush mustache; he was short and rotund, with kind, twinkling brown eyes. He was known more for his compassionate bedside manner than for his medical skills. Dr. Lee said that the documents the girl held noted she was seven years old but did not list the child's birth date or name. There was also information about a trust fund set up for her at a New York bank, by an anonymous benefactor two years earlier. "Someone obviously wanted the child taken care of, but had no wish to take care of her themselves."

The girl's temperature was above 105 degrees, and Dr. Lee ordered the two women to bring him ice and cold water. When he saw the small, raised pink spots on her chest, and heard her groans of agony when he palpitated her abdomen, he diagnosed typhoid fever.

Dr. Lee said that everyone who would need to have contact with the child must be inoculated against the disease, and he would see to that immediately. Meanwhile, he advised the women of the dire state of the child's health and said that there was no real cure to turn the disease around at this stage. The doctor explained that typhoid was extremely contagious, and therefore they could not take other children into the orphanage until the contagion had disappeared completely. Then he looked down at the child's beautiful face and sadly added, "That is, if this little girl survives."

What a blow this was to the staff, which had been so energized to begin their good work! The castle was scheduled to open the very next day, but instead of a grand opening, health officials plastered "Quarantine" notices on the outside of the buildings. All members of the board decided to be inoculated, and although devastated by this crisis, they were one in their decision to stay and help the child. Reinforcing their decision to care for the child was the knowledge that the closest hospital for colored people was many miles away in Atlanta.

Cordelia was especially stunned and disappointed, for she was the energizing voice behind the castle's existence. However, she took care of business as usual, recruiting Springhill Normal School student and faculty volunteers, as well as religious and civic organizations. While they wrote letters of regret to the many agencies that were slated to send orphans to them, Cordelia saw to serving the volunteers meals and refreshments. The young people who worked so energetically in preparing the castle's facilities for the children's arrival were able to express hope for the future through their shared sense of optimism.

As for Alice King, she had spent months planning a smooth opening, and her student teachers from Springhill Normal had undergone several orientation sessions and were eager to begin their duties. Now everything had changed! At first she was in a quandary as to what to do about her daughter, Stacey. Alice finally asked her mother and father to come from Ohio and take Stacey back to the farm with them. After the threat of contagion was over, she told them, Stacy could return. At any rate, Stacey had been pining for Ohio since coming to Springhill and had asked her mother several times if she could go to live with her grandparents.

After Stacey returned to Ohio, Alice funneled all the motherly love that lay within her toward caring for the little one. Alice named her Cleopatra for the queen of Egypt and gave her the last name of Marshall—the head of the procession. During the first months of her life at the empty orphanage, Cleo received the full attention of the newly organized staff, and as she grew stronger, she became their delight.

Miss Rosa, the cook, was her best friend, or at least that's the way Cleo felt about her. When she was well enough to leave her room, she would tiptoe down the long, winding stairs and run to the kitchen, where she would usually find Miss Rosa at the big stove bent over a pot. Miss Rosa smiled whenever she saw her and asked, "How's my sweet little friend today?" Cleo adored her stories, usually about the animals that lived in the woods, while she sat on the high stool by the warm stove, her legs swinging above the floor, nibbling on samples of delectable goodies that came from Rosa's oven. "Jes' for you, my sweetie-pie," Rosa would say.

Cleo loved to watch Miss Rosa stir foods in big, black pots, or toss a piece of dough as if it were a pleasant toy. The aromas of spices and sugar filled her head with visions of delicious food that would soon materialize on her plate. Her favorite food was grated sweet potatoes, a delicacy flavored with cinnamon and brown sugar. Miss Rosa's cheerfulness surrounded Cleo like a soothing hug, and at the end of the day, after she had cleaned the kitchen and put away all the pots, Rosa took her to the big old rocking chair in the corner by the window and sang lullabies to her in her deep, throaty voice, so pleasant to Cleo's ears, like a slow wind blowing through a wet fog.

One day, evening seemed to fall more rapidly, for the air was filled with a light fog, and soft shades of pink and gold filtered downward through the haze. Rosa held Cleo on her lap, rocking back and forth in the big old rocking chair in the kitchen corner. Cleo knew that this meant the end of the day for them both. Cleo sank drowsily against Rosa's bosom, listening as she had so many times before to Rosa's sweet voice singing along with the rocking chair's comforting "rat-tat." She imagined a train rolling slowly along its tracks into a dark tunnel. Instead of caressing her into sleep, the image jarred Cleo awake. "Tell me a story about my mommy," she said.

Rosa was taken aback and fell silent, patting the child's back. Cleo persisted, "Tell me the story of how she fed me by the fire."

Rosa remembered she had told Cleo that during her first months at the orphanage, when Cleo could not keep any food down, Alice King had rocked her by the fire for days, feeding her small spoons of chicken broth in order to build up her strength, until finally she was able to digest Rosa's thick vegetable and chicken soups. Rosa had told her this as Cleo helped her in the kitchen. Now she wondered if she had confused the child. She hugged Cleo tighter, kissing her forehead, and whispered, "It's time for bed. Now close your eyes and I'll sing your favorite song."

Cleo closed her eyes and listened to Rosa's husky voice singing,

"Carry me back to old Virginny, That's where the cotton and the corn and 'tatoes grow ..." Soon Cleo was remembering tastes of corn and sweet potatoes combined with the pine scent of the brightly lit fireplace, and the smell of Mrs. King's toilet water; a scent like lavender flowers with a hint of orange peel.

Whenever Cleo asked Mrs. King about her life as her baby, she would respond with a string of reassuring phrases like "We're so lucky to have you," "Stop worrying your pretty little head about what's past and done with," "The moving finger writes and having writ moves on." Cleo assumed she would find her life's story in writing one day.

During the months she was recovering, Cleo often sat inside her sleeping porch bedroom, her knees on the window seat cushion, her nose pressed to one of the panes of the long row of windows, looking down onto the yard one flight below. She would wave when she saw Mrs. King bringing her frothy glasses of eggnog, and sometimes apples and peaches from her garden, peeled and cut into cubes, or those delectable cream pastries she made just for her. Sometimes watching her walk up the path, a kind of trance overtook Cleo, and she could almost imagine Mrs. King having the wings of an angel bearing her forward, so graceful, serene, and erect she walked. Cleo was happy that Mrs. King wasn't a severe-looking white angel like the one painted on the reception room ceiling.

Finally, Dr. Lee came for the last time to Cleo's bed. He looked into her eyes, pulling them this way and that, as she watched with amusement his large mustache move up and down with each peek. After withdrawing the thermometer from her mouth, he announced to the Wallaces and Alice King, with great certainty, that Cleo had completely recovered and no longer demonstrated any contagion. Although Cleo had no idea what "contagion" meant, she later wished she could bring whatever it was back again and, along with it, the special attention she had received during her illness.

One evening shortly after the doctor assured the staff that Cleo was well, Mrs. King brought a cup of cocoa to her room much later than usual, the aroma rousing Cleo from a sound sleep. Seeking Cleo's sleepy eyes, Mrs. King cooed, "How about some of my cocoa, Sugar? I hope I didn't wake you."

Cleo sat up, all attention and adoration, and said, "No ma'am. I love the cocoa you bring me; it warms my tummy and I can go right to sleep."

"Up you go, then, lean forward now, so I can prop this pillow behind you." Alice crunched a small white pillow behind Cleo's back.

Sitting on the bed, she pulled Cleo toward her, the child's head resting on her shoulder.

As the warm liquid slid down her throat, Cleo's body sank into Mrs. King's large soft breasts. Cleo caressed her bosom and murmured sleepily, "Mama … stay with me tonight. Please Mama!"

Alice abruptly let her go. Standing, looking down at her with concerned eyes, she spoke concisely and firmly.

"Tomorrow you'll meet some new girls who are coming to live here in the castle with you." Her voice was loud, and the cheerfulness sounded forced. "I'll have many girls to take care of, and you'll have many lovely classmates."

Alice moved away, taking some towels and sheets to the other cot and making up the bed. As she moved quickly about the room, she avoided Cleo's searching eyes, and Cleo was filled with a sense of foreboding.

Alice stood near the door and, turning to Cleo with a faint smile, said, "Just imagine how nice it'll be to have other girls to play with. You'll have company in your room at night too, so those bad dreams will soon go away. Good night, Cleo, and pleasant dreams." Alice closed the door softly behind her.

Cleo heard Mrs. King's footsteps echo rapidly away from her down the hall. She asked herself aloud, "Other children? What is she talking about?" Cleo's heart pounded like booted sentinels marching across her chest. She covered her mouth to prevent the scream that begged for release.

CHAPTER FOUR

CLEO AWOKE TO THE bright light invading her room. Her curtains, usually closed, had been left open, and the sun shone with a light so intense and colorful that it made a rainbow on the walls of her room—a good omen, she hoped. But as Cleo washed in the bathroom and rubbed herself dry, tears stung her eyes and ran unrelentingly down her flushed cheeks. She licked away the salty tears and threw handfuls of cold water in her face. Then she dressed and went down to breakfast.

As Mrs. King had promised, there were seven new girls in the reception hall. Mrs. King introduced Cleo to the other girls, saying, "This is the very first little girl to come to this beautiful castle. She's been waiting a long time for all of you to arrive." Mrs. King smiled and nodded toward Cleo. They were all standing around the fireplace in a circle, and Cleo longed for Mrs. King to hold her hand, but she made no such gesture.

The seven girls stared at Cleo. Cleo looked shyly at them and gave a little bow, clutching the skirt of her uniform, looking curiously at the identically dressed girls. They stood in a row, all different sizes, and Cleo was asked to tell them her name and then they would introduce themselves. Cleo struggled with the visions in red, green, and white flashing about her, for each one was dressed in the red and green pleated skirt, white blouse, and green vest that she also wore. She had adored this outfit when she found it on her chair, thinking it was a special present for her. When the ordeal of introductions was over, Mrs. King led them into the big dining room instead of the small breakfast room off the kitchen. Mrs. Wallace and Mrs. King stood at opposite ends of the long pine table in the main dining room, their hands resting on the top of high-backed chairs.

Finally, Mrs. King said to her attentive little audience, "Now, find your names at the table—that's right, just walk around until you see your name on a chair, and that will be your seat from now on."

Mrs. King smiled and nodded, as the children marched around until all had found their seats.

"You did that well, thank you. You may be seated. I want to remind you that during meals, there will be no talking unless you are experiencing some kind of immediate difficulty. If and when such a situation occurs you may say, 'Excuse me, Mrs. King,' or 'Excuse me, Mrs. Wallace.'" She motioned with an outstretched arm toward the woman at the other end of the table. "Then you may state your concern or emergency. Is that understood? Another rule is that you must be polite to everyone, not only to all adults, but to each of your classmates as well. This courtesy is to be practiced at all times. Is that understood? Well then, Mrs. Wallace, is there anything you would like to add?"

"Thank you, Mrs. King. Young ladies, I am chairman of the board of directors of the castle. Welcome to your new home!"

The shorter girls sat on large library books to boost them up. Cleo didn't quite know what to make of these girls, dark-skinned and somber, most of them at least two or three years younger than she.

Alice King was looking from one to the other around the table, speaking in a formal tone instead of her usual voice. "Cleo, will you come forward and tell the new girls the rituals we complete before we begin eating?"

Cleo rose quickly and came forward, standing beside Mrs. King.

"Cleo, will you tell us what is the very first thing we do before we can begin a meal?"

After a moment of collecting herself, a bit uneasy but proud of her leadership role, Cleo spoke in a loud, clear, commanding voice that she hoped would impress all the new children. "We say the blessing. No, sorry," Cleo blushed and looked down before continuing, "the first thing we do is put our hands together, like this, and hold them that way until we finish the blessing. Then, we say together, 'God is great, God is good, and we thank him for this food. Amen.'"

"Thank you, Cleo, and what do we do next?" Mrs. King asked, casting an admiring smile toward her.

This bolstered her spirit so much that Cleo squared her shoulders and lifted her chin as she continued. "We stand and look up at the angel on the ceiling and say, 'Thank you, angel, for watching over us and keeping us from harm.' And then we look at the painting over the fireplace."

All the girls' eyes turned to the painting of a handsome white man on horseback. The girls followed Cleo's lead as she said, "Thank you, Mr. Treadwell, for your gift of this home."

Cleo's body trembled, as usual, when she looked into the glaring horse's bloodshot, wild eye, with Mr. Treadwell atop its broad back. *Control yourself,* she thought. This time he didn't take his derby hat off and tip it toward her, as he often did when she looked at him. She looked quickly away from the painting.

When Cleo completed her treatise on the use of napkins, utensils, and the practice of mealtime etiquette, the children finally bowed their heads and repeated the blessing. Cleo felt proud of being a leader and began, for the first time, to relish being a "big sister."

Cleo looked around the table at the other children, and although she felt proud to be older than the others, she knew without being told that she would never again sit by the stove in the kitchen with Miss Rosa all to herself, warm and happy, with the smells of bread and spices mingling with the sounds of the women's laughter and chatter. The women served the plates of food and passed them down the table. But even the smell of this food caused Cleo to turn her head away, for she did not want any of it.

The strange girls were eating hungrily, their heads practically in their plates, gulping down large quantities of food, bits of juices dribbling in ugly stains down their chins, yet neither Mrs. King nor Mrs. Wallace said anything to them. They just smiled and appeared completely happy with these girls' abominable manners.

Then Alice King rang a little bell at her fingertips, and with so much excitement in her voice that it riveted everyone to instant attention, she said, "Oh, girls! I have some wonderful news. My daughter arrives from Cleveland this evening. She has been away for the summer visiting her grandparents in Ohio and will be attending classes with us."

Mrs. King looked around at the girls, smiling widely, bringing her hands together in a gleeful silent clap, her usual dignity having all but disappeared. Looking at Mrs. King's animated countenance, the girls' faces broke into wide grins—all of the girls except Cleo. She was staring at Mrs. King with horror and disbelief. She felt utterly betrayed that her "mother" had a daughter that she had never mentioned to her, and that she was coming here to the castle. A choking sensation rose in her throat. She pressed her mouth into her napkin, to prohibit the upward passage of a piece of biscuit.

After breakfast, Alice and Cordelia led the children to the library. Cleo heard Mrs. King whispering, "Isn't it nice that Cleo is well again! I'm so glad we are finally free of that awful contagion at last."

Even though Mrs. King had spoken in a somewhat hushed tone, some of the girls suddenly turned toward Cleo, curiosity written all over their faces. When they were seated, Cleo, red-faced, looked down at her hands, thinking, *All the children will think I am dirty and disgusting. They will be afraid to be near me.*

Life had seemed safe and good, but suddenly everything had changed. Cleo knew Mrs. King was not her mother; this place was not her home, and these knock-kneed, kinky-haired, ashy-faced girls were all cast-offs, like herself, hated and despised by mothers, unknown to fathers, with no sisters, brothers, or any kinfolk. And when she realized she could never change things back, her heart broke.

CHAPTER FIVE

CLEO WAS TOLD THAT since she was the oldest, she would share a room with just one other girl, while most of the children slept four to a room. Edna had been chosen as her roommate. She had wanted to get to know Edna better from the moment Edna had smiled at her and put her hands together as if to clap when she finished her speech at breakfast. Edna's admiring eyes were the only bright spot in the day so far. She was the only girl who showed her any signs of friendliness. Cleo said a silent prayer of gratitude, for she was terrified of most of these children, who seemed to her poor and ill mannered. Now a cloud descended over her as she worried that Edna might have heard of her contagion and would also most likely be afraid of her. However, when Cleo looked at her, Edna's face lit up with a wide, inviting smile.

Later, when they had free time, Cleo and Edna walked hand-in-hand to their room, the brightest and most cheerful bedroom, the sleeping porch that had been selected by the staff in order to give Cleo the advantage of sunlight and fresh air during her illness.

In the afternoon, all the girls were led on a tour of the castle and a stroll on the grounds. Several men working on the property, who usually kept their eyes averted when Cleo passed alone, looked up in surprise when they saw a group of girls, for the men lived in town and had not noticed their arrival. The buildings close by were occupied by female staff and the women who worked at the castle—cooks, maids, laundresses, teachers, and of course, Alice King. The girls were warned not to walk about alone, nor go near the springs or any other body of water without a staff member accompanying them.

As Cleo strolled along with Edna at her side, she was surprised by the younger girl's happiness in being a resident at the castle. Edna gushed on with enthusiasm about her great luck in being here, and her hope that this would be the last home of the many in which she had spent brief stays. Cleo searched her mind to find a new perspective for her view of "home." Until a short time ago, she had indeed thought the castle was hers, Alice King her mother, and the servants hired to cater to her.

Toward the end of their walk, Cleo and Edna sat on a bench in the main garden near the castle's entrance. Cleo was startled by the question that Edna then asked her. She asked where she had lived before she came to the castle and who her parents were. Cleo quickly improvised a response. "It's a very long story, and there are a lot of twists and turns in it. It's a fairy tale, sort of, except that it's real. But first, you have to promise you won't tell anyone, because it's a secret. And it's a secret that must be sealed with blood. So we'll have to cut our fingers. Maybe that won't be enough blood," she warned. "Maybe we'll have to cut our wrists."

Edna seemed excited by this mystery, as if it confirmed Cleo's glamour and allure. She promised Cleo she would keep her secret but explained, "I'll wait until I'm older, because right now I'm afraid of the sight of blood."

Edna seemed impressed that an older girl would spend time with her. Cleo, for her part, was delighted to have made friends with a girl so lively and energetic, a sweet, honest, and bright little girl with whom she hoped she might one day share everything. She had never had a relationship like that in her life, and she was both repelled and drawn by its possibilities.

Edna habitually left her own bed at night and snuggled up to Cleo. Even though Edna was thin as a stick, her muscles were obviously strong. She outperformed all the other girls in athletic games that required running, jumping, and climbing. One night as they lay in bed together, Edna told Cleo that she had almost starved to death as a baby. She had survived several foster-care farms, having been passed around and traded off for orphaned boys who came by train from the Northeast to work the farms of the Midwest. Her own father had left the family to travel to Chicago looking for work when she was two and was never heard from again. Shortly afterward, her mother was taken to a hospital where, within a few weeks, she died. Her aunt, poor and overburdened with her own five mouths to feed, took Edna to the social welfare people and asked for temporary foster care, which turned into months, and then years. To Edna, the castle was like a fairyland and the people who ran it were the best of "mothers." Edna's positive attitude, and her friendship with Cleo, helped her become popular with most of the girls at the castle.

One day there was a different seating arrangement, for a new group of children had arrived. Cleo was seated at a table with Stacey King on her left and Ophelia Wallace, Mrs. Wallace's daughter, on her right. Cleo felt irritable and confused with the constant changes of children and thought it was cruel that they would surround her with girls who had their own mothers. When dinner was over, the women shepherded the girls who had just arrived into chairs near the fire in the reception room. As they sat together in a circle, the new girls were asked to tell about their train trip to the castle and about their summer adventures.

Stacey boasted, "I had so much fun with my grandfather, who taught me to ride a pony. He has a big farm with lots of horses and when I'm bigger he's gonna let me ride them; maybe even give me my very own horse. He's rich and has a big farm."

Everyone stared at her with mean eyes behind sad faces, then at Mrs. King, as if this haughty and annoying child had been brought forth by her to deliberately inflict misery upon them. Cleo felt a lump that started in her throat and fell suddenly into the depths of her stomach.

Noticing Cleo's anxious look, Mrs. King said, "Cleo, why don't you, Edna, and Stacey go to our game corner and choose a game to play." Stacey and Edna stood at once, but Cleo sat and continued to stare at the floor until Edna pulled her from her chair. Stacey ran in front of Cleo, taunting her, "Hey, ugly, my mother told me she had to bring you food every day when you first came because you were so sickly she was afraid you were gonna to die."

She took a few menacing steps around Cleo and said, pulling one long pigtail and shaking it toward her, "When you were born, you were so-o-o ugly and trashy looking even your own mother deserted you." Her voice was high and shrill, and her slanted black eyes shone with mischief. She cackled an evil laugh, like wind blowing on dry leaves.

Cleo drew her body up to its full height, a good three inches above Stacey's, and looking down into her dark, teasing eyes proclaimed haughtily, "My mother was a princess who lived in this very castle a long time ago. Bad soldiers kidnapped her. But when she gets loose, she's coming back to get me. So, you don't know what you're talking about. That's a secret not even your mother knows."

Stacey moved past them, and Edna took Cleo's hand and whispered, "Don't pay her any mind. She's stupid and tells lies." Edna pulled Cleo along and added, "When she first saw me, she came right over to me and said I was a witch's daughter, because my hair was standing straight up. She thinks she's something 'cause her mother is in charge here."

Cleo had believed for a long time that Mrs. King was her mother. It somehow remained a fuzzy possibility in her head. After Stacey's tirade, however, she remembered again how far from reality she had let herself wander in those days.

"We belong to no one," Cleo said aloud.

"Maybe we can belong here," Edna replied.

Stacey seemed the one least deserving of the good fortune to belong to someone—especially someone as pretty and lovely as Mrs. King. Stacey and her mother lived in their own house down a path directly across from Cleo and Edna's second-floor bedroom.

Later, Cleo sat on the window seat in her room, her eyes glancing away from her book, toward Stacey skipping rope to a steady beat up and down the path that separated her cottage from their building. Cleo's face burned with fury as she watched Stacey's braids flying in the wind, her long, skinny legs beating a perfect rhythm. Stacey could go home and play after classes were over, while the other girls performed chores such as helping the cook, washing dishes, setting the tables, and dusting and polishing the furniture in the living areas.

CHAPTER SIX

I N CLEO'S DREAM, THE hall was vast but somehow more confining than in recent memory. The usually clean white walls were covered with streaks of red, perhaps paint or crayon—smeared hand-marks suggesting a child's malicious activities. As she listened closely, she could hear whispering sounds around her, but she couldn't make out what they were saying. She pressed her ears to the wall, and the sounds disappeared. She was compelled to move down the stairs. There was urgency to her mission, but she didn't yet know what she must do. Her shadow on the walls followed her like an uninvited dance partner, both comforting and terrifying, as she hurried down the stairs, which seemed to never end. The dark shadows gathered silently behind her; she heard only her own raspy breath. She saw light ahead and moved toward it.

Running swiftly through the dining room, Cleo found herself confronting an immense fireplace. As she had done many times in the past, she dared herself to pause and study the large painting above the slate mantel. Again she cringed at the horse's fiery eye staring down at her—an eye like a deep, dangerous cavern. He stood as still as a statue, and on his huge back a rider was seated, his face partially obscured by a large black sombrero. Cleo moved slowly into the reception room, forcing her eyes upward toward the ceiling fresco, where a severe white angel blessed the disheveled multitude below as they ran to escape the pursuing reach of blood-covered waters.

Cleo rushed to the heavy, arched door and grabbed the doorknob, pushing, tugging, using both hands at once trying to turn it, but it didn't budge. She screamed, yet no sound came. Remembering, she turned toward the familiar scarred antique desk to the left of the door. She opened a drawer and removed a huge key that seemed almost too heavy for her hands to lift. She unlocked the door and stepped out. Once outside, the breeze enveloped her and carried her forward. The door slammed behind her. As her bare feet touched the cold cement, she fell back against the door. A piercing stab moved like an invisible arrow through her head, and she crumbled onto herself.

Later, Cleo had no idea how long, her eyes opened to a full moon overhead, trees moving in time to a balmy summer breeze. An uncanny calmness permeated the air. Yet the trees and the flowers around her seemed shrouded in a mist; everything appeared out of focus. Why was she lingering here on the stoop against the closed door in her cotton nightgown?

Tears suddenly filled her eyes as she clenched her fists in despair, muttering aloud, "I've been sleepwalking again." A disturbing new awareness entered her consciousness: "But I never walked *outside* before. How could I get out of a locked door?" She knew there were no unlocked doors or windows because the staff double-checked, even triple-checked the locks at every entrance before bedtime.

Now, everyone will know I'm not a normal person—not a normal girl, she thought. Cleo made a vain attempt to open the door, but it had locked securely behind her. Finally, she crept down onto the grass past the evergreens that bordered the front path and saw her favorite tree, a giant magnolia a few steps away. She pulled her gown around her more tightly and ran to the spot where she often escaped the noisy clamor of the younger children during their playtime. As she curled up under the magnolia's sheltering branches and watched the moonlight's rays illuminating the upright cups of its blossoms, she began to feel more at ease. Cleo lay on her back and breathed in deeply its soothing aroma, gazing up through the blossoms to the dark azure sky where the full moon floated like a magical balloon on a vast upside-down sea. While praying for protection from ghosts, snakes, lizards, spiders, and the unknown, Cleo fell asleep on the mossy earth.

Cleo awakened and bolted upright as the bright sunshine blurred her vision so she could barely make out the moving figure coming toward her. Mrs. Wallace walked jauntily up the path in a bouncy familiar stride, but today there seemed an urgent determination to her posture, as if she were being blown forward by a strong wind. Cleo's instant happiness at the sight of Cordelia, who had always come to her aid in times of trouble, was tinged with panic. "What if she thinks I'm crazy? The Wallaces may never invite me to their house again. They may never let me play games with their children." The pleasant memories of afternoons spent in the Wallace home were pulled apart as she saw her hopes of being with a real family dwindling before her eyes. Covered with moss and sticks, Cleo ran out to the path and quickly up the stone steps as if to block Mrs. Wallace's entrance. Cordelia gathered the trembling girl to her, brushing away the grasses that clung to Cleo's long cotton gown, repeating over and over, "It's all right, dear. Let me hold you and warm you. Everything is going to be all right."

Finally, after Cleo had calmed somewhat, Cordelia took a deep breath and looked into the girl's dark, perplexed eyes. She asked, "Why are you out here? What on earth happened?"

Cleo faced Cordelia Wallace tearfully, not knowing how to answer her questions. Cleo cried, "I don't know, I don't know what happened!" She leaned against Cordelia, burying her face against her soft knit jacket, wishing she could hide forever in her embrace.

Cordelia bent down and looked into Cleo's teary, frightened eyes. "Are you all right? I mean, physically all right? Did anyone hurt you?"

Cleo cried, "No, no, I just came out the door in my sleep and it slammed shut behind me, and I couldn't get back in, so I lay down under the magnolia tree. I think the mourning dove woke me up once at dawn, but I went back to sleep again, and then the sun came up. And I saw you coming, and …" Her voice turned into a whimper.

Cordelia lifted Cleo's chin gently and said in a voice, both consoling and firm, "Then, I think we had better go inside now and let everyone know you're all right."

Cordelia moved a step up to the door, pulling Cleo with her, arms still around her shoulders, and lifted the large brass knocker. She asked, "Did you perhaps have a bad dream?"

Cleo was so grateful for this idea—everyone has bad dreams—that she walked in, her mood considerably brighter. But once inside, as she looked toward the large dining hall and saw the other girls, her courage waned.

Cordelia steered Cleo toward a stairway off the entrance hall. "Cleo, I think you need to rest. Why don't you go back to bed for a nap, and I'll bring you up a breakfast tray."

Alice King had watched them come in. Attempting to distract everyone's attention, she walked into the kitchen and came around to the front hall through a butler's pantry, joining them at the foot of the winding staircase.

Alice put her finger to her lips, whispering to Cordelia, "Thanks for coming so quickly. Could you see she is attended to? I don't want to alert the others."

As Alice returned to the dining room, she wondered if anyone had missed Cleo and thought it was unlikely, considering the time of day and the fact that everyone knew Cleo often spent nights at the Wallace home. Alice thought of all the things she had to get done today. And now this! The most important task was to call Dr. Lee just to cover her back. Who knows what could happen to a girl out in the woods all night? This was probably another episode of sleepwalking. It was never considered too big a problem before, as she never harmed anything and had never before walked outside. Now it was different. One day she might wander deep into the woods surrounding this vast acreage and be attacked by man or beast, and that would be the end of their dreams and all they had tried so hard to accomplish here.

Cordelia remained through Dr. Lee's quick examination and was relieved that Cleo had not been harmed. She had hoped Cleo would outgrow her disorder, but now she was genuinely fearful for her future. As Cordelia sat by her bed watching the interplay of conflicting emotions flitting across the girl's face as she slept, she yearned to do more to help her. She was like one of the family, spending most weekends with them, teaching the children games and helping with their schoolwork.

After breakfast, Alice recruited one of the students to take care of her class and slipped upstairs to Cleo's room. Cleo was fast asleep, and Cordelia sat in an upright wooden chair pulled close to the bed, watching her intently. When Alice came in, they both moved over to the window seat so they could talk without disturbing her.

Alice put her arms around Cordelia's shoulders and whispered, "Thank you so much. I'm sorry I woke you up so early. I hope I didn't disturb Albert and the children, but I was terrified! I couldn't call the police—those Ku-Klux-Klanners! They already want to close us down because they think we're putting 'spells' on the girls just because we've taught them to speak good English."

Cordelia replied, "Yes, I think everything turned out okay. Dr. Lee found she was intact, there's not a scratch on her body. He's known about her nightmares and sleepwalking since she came here, and he said this is just another episode."

The two women were silent for a while as Cleo stirred, turned over, and then continued sleeping. Alice asked Cordelia if she had ever heard of a cure for sleepwalking.

"When I was in Paris as Portia Pittman's chaperone, there was a Dr. Sigmund Freud who believed analyzing patients' dreams might help. But I think most doctors now say children usually outgrow the disorder."

Alice watched Cordelia leave the room and gazed out the window to the path below that led to her own small cottage. She was overcome by a great weight bearing down on her and sank to the pillows on the window seat, wondering if she had the energy for all the crises that constantly surrounded them in this place to which she had blindly followed the Wallaces in search of their utopian dream. She walked over to the bed and pulled a blanket around Cleo before leaving the room.

As soon as Alice had gone, Cleo opened her eyes. She had pretended to be asleep but had heard some of the conversation between Mrs. King and Mrs. Wallace about finding a cure for her sleepwalking, and her heart had galloped like frightened horses so that she thought anyone in the room might hear. She had lain there with closed eyes and prayed that something would cure her. She had prayed so many times to be a normal girl, like everybody else, without receiving any sign in return. She wondered what kind of curse God had placed on her.

Cleo pretended she was too sick to go to music class, and indeed she was, but more in mind than body, for she was sure she must be crazy. She had once seen what people called an insane asylum way up on a hill but could not remember when or where. She only remembered riding in a car—or was it a train—next to a large building, and she had looked up at its crumbling facade, so close she could hear the screaming of the tortured people inside. "Is that where they would take me?" She decided she would run away and drown herself in the river before she would go there.

By five o'clock, Cleo's hunger drove her to the dining room, even though she was concerned about what everyone would think of her. When Cleo entered the dining room, the teachers looked up as if nothing unusual had occurred and continued eating. The girls, however, gave her furtive glances, but even that was not unusual. After all, she was a little late, and that was against the rules. But Cleo was frightened by the possibility of punishment that she was certain lay ahead. Mrs. King and Mrs. Wallace came into the dining room, speaking animatedly to each other. They both laughed, and seeing this, Cleo was relieved.

She attempted to calm her wildly beating heart by recalling a cheerful memory of her own. Cleo thought of her dancing lessons with Gwendolyn Redd, her history teacher's daughter, who had recently come from Chicago. She was young and let the girls call her by her first name—Gwen. After her first lesson, Gwen had given Cleo a glossy book with huge black-and-white photographs of London's Vic Welles'

Ballet, which she had kept safe under her mattress ever since. Many nights she looked at the pictures and imagined herself as the principal ballerina, especially after Gwen had shown her photographs of a young, beautiful Negro ballet dancer named Katherine Dunham. After only her third dance lesson, Gwen told Cleo she had the body, posture, and soul of a dancer, and she would be a great ballerina some day.

Whenever she was sad and that awful feeling came over her, like an empty hole aching to be filled, a favorite thought usually cheered her: "When I get to be sixteen, I'm going to leave this place and become a dancer in the *Ballet Russe*." And at that very moment a vision appeared, as the lead dancer's body moved gracefully before her eyes, and then the face and body faded into her own, with her dark hair done up in a pompadour held back by a crown of roses. She is twirling around the room, as the arms of a strong, dark, handsome man circles her waist and lifts her high above his head. She is ever so graceful and erect, her arms outstretched as if to reach the array of rainbow-colored banners hanging from the majestically carved ceiling. Her legs are extended, toes pointed, and then she is descending, weightlessly floating down to the stage. The audience's thunderous applause is loud in her ears as she performs her curtsy.

The hand on her shoulder startled Cleo just as she was about to take her bow. Mrs. King was saying something to her, her voice calm, with a rather perplexed look in her eyes. Cleo jumped from her seat and said, "I'm sorry, ma'am, I didn't hear you."

Mrs. King said kindly, "I'm so glad to see you up. Mrs. Wallace was very disappointed when you missed her class. I'll tell her you're okay. Try to read a few pages of the book I left by your bed. You slept so long today you might not get to sleep right away tonight. So *Jane Eyre* can keep you company until you fall asleep."

CHAPTER SEVEN

A T AGE TWELVE, CLEO stood out because she was one of the most popular and influential girls at the castle. But, at the same time, she was most often rejected for adoption because she had unique features. In the old days they might have called her "mulatto," but now they used terms like "mixed" or "half-breed," not that anyone knew anything certain about her background. Most Negro families did not want to adopt such a light-skinned child. Cordelia had talked with Albert about legally adopting Cleo long ago, but although he approved of her frequent visits, he was adamantly against it. Some of the families they approached on Cleo's behalf weren't impressed that she was a studious child either, thinking that an intelligent girl would fancy books instead of housework. Another detriment in placing Cleo was the necessity of disclosing her medical history—her amnesia— and now this instance of somnambulism. Most had no tolerance for children with symptoms of emotional instability.

Over the years Cleo found many ways to coexist comfortably with the children who came and went, and accepted the fact that she was a permanent guest. When Cleo asked Mrs. King why no one wanted her, Alice told her that it was just that she was older and most people wanted to take younger children. Some of the other girls said to her face that people didn't like her light skin color.

After a while, Cleo rationalized that she belonged to this place and accepted as blessings what she had once seen as curses. She still cringed when she thought about the humiliation of having families look her over as if she were a slab of meat. As was the custom, the girls being interviewed for adoption were sent alone to a room with the potential adoptive parents.

Cleo never forgot the Sunday afternoon visit by a couple whose interview actions were the scariest of all that remained locked in her memory. Cleo sat on the hard bench between Reverend and Mrs. Dawson. The wife was a very thin, silent woman, who sat staring off into space with a grim expression. Mrs. Dawson was so straight and still, she reminded Cleo of a papier-mâché statue held together by a series of wires.

The man, fat and pudgy, with features resembling a pig's, drew her close, his sweaty palms on her bare arms, and said, "You're a lucky girl because you're so pretty, so delectable." He smelled bad, like old, sour sweat that had oozed out of his skin and taken up permanent residence in his moldy dress clothes. He held her left hand in his, while his wife inched steadily away from her. Then his clumsy hands were on her thighs, pretending to smooth her thin organdie dress, and her legs became increasingly damp with his sweat.

Cleo wanted to scream at the woman to make her husband take his hands off her. But his wife sat looking away, appearing as paralyzed by her husband's actions as Cleo was. Noting the tears that escaped from Cleo's eyes, he thrust his pig face in front of hers and said, "Now there, my child, you'll soon be leaving this place and coming home with us." He wiped the tears away with his scaly thumb, saying in a fake, consoling voice, "How can a girl so beautiful be so unhappy? God loves you, and so do the missus and me. You are the only girl we want." He continued his low, purring sounds, as he slid his arm around her, his hand underneath her arm, pulling her closer while his fingers crept toward her breast. Cleo inched closer to Mrs. Dawson, who moved farther away.

The Reverend's purr became a growl, "What's wrong with you, child? Do you know what's gonna happen to you when they close this place and throw you out in the street? The men out there will pick you apart like vultures trying to get at you. You better thank God that he sent us to protect you!"

When Cleo buried her face in her hands and sobbed aloud, Reverend Dawson attempted to crush her shaking shoulders, grasping her body with both arms and saying, "What's your problem? You think you're too good for us because your skin is high yellow?"

Before she even realized what she'd done, Cleo had elbowed him in the ribs. The Reverend recoiled, rage in his pig eyes. "Why you little—"

Terrified, Cleo ran screaming from the room. When the women outside heard her screams, they rose quickly and caught Cleo in their arms, comforting her with soft reassurances as others led the irate minister and his wife to the door.

After a number of frightening encounters with "potential parents," Cleo never complained again about not being adopted. She forgot the Reverend's ominous warnings of being thrown out on the streets and instead embraced the castle as her home. Cleo appreciated its rules and rituals, because she could be certain how each day would unfold, and that added to her sense of security. She enjoyed her designated place at the dining table on the right hand of the head teacher of the day, and she was the person the faculty always chose to teach the new arrivals about the rules of conduct, courtesy, dining, study, and chores.

Cleo loved the castle's beautiful grounds, and nature's bountiful trees, flowers, and fields brought her a sense of serenity. She and Edna had long ago settled in as roommates, and she loved her. She loved her adoring eyes, her skin like dark velvet, and most of all, her sense of humor. Edna made her laugh even during those times when she was on the verge of tears. Sometimes she resented Edna's eternal optimism, for it often felt like the sun bursting through a black cloud when what she wanted was a little rain.

CHAPTER EIGHT

UMULUS CLOUDS MOVED ACROSS the sky like sailboats on a blue sea. It was a hot spring day in 1932. Fourteen girls stood on the banks of the crystal clear waters below the sandstone cliffs. Alice and Cordelia were marveling at the flowered smocks the girls wore and their brightly colored hair ribbons waving gently in the breeze. With the cliffs and the clear spring waters behind them, the girls began their dance. And Alice and Cordelia almost wished for a camera or paintbrush to record the bucolic scene, capturing for perpetuity the children's carefree frolics, for they feared this May Day might be their last.

The staff was relieved that this day was one of the most beautiful ever, though a rain cloud had flaunted its threatening presence earlier. As the crowd looked westward toward the castle on the hill, they might be reminded of pictures of foreign places, scenes in other countries— never here in a downtrodden corner of Georgia. Newcomers among the invited guests asked how the staff had selected such well-cared-for, graceful, and immaculately dressed colored schoolgirls. The faculty members were too caring to say, "You should have seen them when they arrived."

The adult volunteer staff had put all their skills into the planning of this May Day celebration to raise money, because the castle's very existence was in jeopardy. Picnic tables were laden with potato salad, tiny sandwiches with the crusts removed, a flank of sliced ham and one of lamb, blackberry and sweet potato pies, lemonade, and Kool-Aid. The girls had made the flower wreaths for their hair, the Maypole ribbons, and banners. The Springhill College string quintet's rendition of Chopin waltzes floated aloft in the breeze. Oscar, the Wallaces' son, now fourteen, was the leader of the jazz trio scheduled to play later. Ophelia, twelve, his sister, was the featured singer. Cleo was sixteen and her best friend, Edna, had just turned fourteen—ages when the girls became "big sisters," each in charge of a group of younger girls whom they supervised during play and story times. Cleo and Edna were also in charge of these May Day activities, a major holiday event of the year. Cleo designed the costumes and taught the children several dances. Edna helped in making and arranging the table decorations.

After the children's performances were over, the orchestra continued to play a short program, creating a pleasant aura of relaxed comfort for the gorgeously attired guests strolling the lawns, sitting on benches in the parklike setting, or lingering on blankets spread out on the grass.

Cleo was irritable today, having worked tirelessly with a new group of difficult students in putting on this pageant. Her solace as usual was Edna, forever at her side. Yesterday, one of the girls, jealous of Cleo's authority, ripped up some of the costumes she had designed, and Cleo had worked late into the night to mend the outfits.

Now, Cleo yearned for privacy and peace, even from Edna. She needed some time to stroll alone like the others walking so blissfully around the grounds, so she asked Edna to take charge of the circle games, and she slipped silently away.

Cleo walked a good distance from the springs and wandered into the woods. Afterward, enthralled with the beauty of a meadow in a circle of dogwood trees, she stopped to pick some blossoming larkspur and blue flags for the dinner table. She soon realized she had wandered off the path. She gazed upward through the trees, and a flash of light caught the corner of her eye but disappeared just as quickly. She walked in that direction, and the flash suddenly returned—but again disappeared.

What is that? she asked herself. Thinking it might be coming from the castle, Cleo rushed forward, following the flashes of light. Suddenly, she saw a man—the tallest man she had ever seen—standing at an easel painting pictures on glass. A pane of painted glass was hanging from the tree, flashing as it swung back and forth in the breeze.

The man turned to her, and even though she wanted to run, no part of her body would move. Her heart thudded so loudly, she felt as if it would burst through her chest. He came forward, a bronze-skinned giant, his long dark hair slicked back and tied in a ponytail, his narrow eyes and glistening white teeth forming into an amused smile.

In a deep, sonorous voice that seemed to come from a long distance away, he said, "Hey, what do we have here? You lost, honey?" Seeing her fear, he added, "Don't be afraid, I'm not going to hurt you." He knelt and held his hand out, palm up, as one would calm a pet. "Honey, I know the whole of these woods; I can lead you safely home. Tell Mister Isaac where you live."

Cleo did not hear another word. Throwing the flowers at him, she screamed and scrambled away, tripping and falling several times, rushing, leaping, and jumping over stumps and fallen trees she hadn't noticed before. As an eerie silence surrounded her and dark shadows loomed, she knew she was lost.

After taking several different paths and then retreating, Cleo was unable to see anything for the dense foliage and tall trees. She was afraid of the consequences of calling out for help. The sun cast a surreal light through the branches as Cleo searched about to get her bearings, while a jumble of thoughts rushed through her head: *Did I really see a man? Am I dreaming? Did I see God?*

At that moment, she heard the sound of the springs and, following it, finally saw the castle's tower once again in the distant hills. When she reached the picnic spot, the sun was descending, its rays slowly moving away through the trees. Everyone was gone, and the springs looked like silver platters, tree branches reflected like massive wreaths on its flat surface.

Cleo finally heard several of the teachers calling her name and ran toward them with open arms. Alice and Cordelia looked at her disheveled state and rushed Cleo inside, taking her to her room. They called Nurse Lee, who came immediately.

As Nurse Lee, with Cordelia's aid, attended to her cuts and bruises, Cleo lay on her bed silent and trembling, afraid to reveal what she now believed to be a figment of her imagination—a giant in the woods. Fearing that her sleepwalking illness had returned, she pretended to be exhausted, and the women had no choice but to abandon their questions until a later time.

Cleo was told she would have to remain in her room without supper as punishment for leaving the group.

Edna volunteered to stay with Cleo, and as soon as they were alone, she climbed into Cleo's small narrow bed, placing her arms around her. Cleo, wide awake now, was staring into the shadows with haunted eyes. Edna was burning with curiosity, but instead of asking questions, she stroked her friend's hair and said, "Are you hungry? I'll go down and steal some of those rolls we had for supper from the kitchen."

Cleo shook her head, "No, you'll get in trouble, and there's no need for us both to be in the doghouse. Edna, I want to tell you something, but you have to promise not to tell a soul."

"Of course, I promise," Edna said eagerly. "We're blood sisters. You know I always keep your secrets."

Cleo trusted Edna. She was the only one who knew Cleo still had recurring nightmares but had never mentioned it to anyone.

"I think I may have been sleepwalking again. I was lost in the woods and I saw an enormous man, standing alone in a clearing. He was beautiful and terrifying, like God. He reached out to me, and I ran."

Edna looked at her with disbelief and said, "You saw the giant. Haven't you ever heard of the giant? Stacey told me about him years ago. He lives on the other side of the woods."

Cleo was overcome with relief. "You mean to tell me he's actually real? I wasn't dreaming it?" She jumped out of bed, and pulling Edna to her feet, they danced around the room singing made-up rhymes about a girl who brings flowers to a giant who lives in the woods. Finally, they lay on the floor laughing.

Cleo seldom disobeyed the rules, although her adventurous nature caused her teachers to admonish her from time to time. She was their top student. In fact, Cleo was paid to tutor the children, not only at the orphanage but also at Springhill Normal. At the age of sixteen, she was older and taller than most of the other girls. She was also an accomplished dancer, having continued her lessons with Gwen over several years.

Later that summer, on a perfect evening for the castle's semi-annual gala dinner concert, a large group of well-dressed Negroes gathered around an outdoor stage. This dance concert featured the Oscar Wallace Trio with Cleo as its principal dancer. The concert opened with the band's jazzy rendition of "All God's Chill'en Got Wings." Oscar played rifts on his saxophone and was well received. But most were waiting for Cleo.

Finally the orchestra paused, and Cleo walked gracefully to the center of the stage, a dazzling apparition in white and gold. She turned toward the audience as the music's refrains sounded. Cleo wore a sleeveless, white flimsy dress of her own creation, with a tight bodice and flowing skirt. She held a sheer, long, gold-hued scarf that shimmered to the floor. As the saxophone's "St. Louis Blues" resonated through the air, Cleo danced an adagio, wearing the scarf and caressing it, as if remembering a long-lost lover. A series of haphazard minor notes intruded, as she cast the scarf to the floor with a few kicks and stomps, indicating a romance turned sour. Oscar's saxophone wailed mournfully, while Cleo's dance suggested themes of freedom, pain, loneliness, and love, which drove the audience into a spellbound frenzy.

There was more to Cleo's pleasure than receiving the audience's approval. Whenever she danced, she felt alive and complete as at no other time. Dancing validated her existence and was the source of her affirmation. It was her means of survival and her only authentic joy. She felt as if she were in flight toward a bright and secure galaxy. She was free, a celestial being with no bodily inhibitions, and her everyday doubts and worries melted away like a fiery sun melts snow in winter. Finally, after a series of leaps on a stage white-washed with light, Cleo danced victoriously, waving the scarf like a flag of victory. Then, as the sax descended into its lowest register, Cleo walked defiantly off the stage, head high, scarf streaming along behind her. She returned to bow several times to the audience's thunderous applause. Cleo and Oscar exchanged a long, triumphant look.

When Oscar came home from the prestigious Negro boarding school his parents had sent him to in Atlanta, he was happy to find Cleo very much a part of the family. He had always had a crush on her but imagined a girl like Cleo could get anyone she wanted. He was younger than she, and Cleo had always treated him like a child. He had long since given up trying to impress her, accepting the fact that he was destined to be just her "little brother." But after witnessing Cleo's performance, Oscar was more attracted to her than at any previous time. The last time he had seen her dance was at that church affair where she played the part of Eve to his Adam. But they were both much younger then. Oscar remembered the time she had given him a hug, putting her arms around his shoulders, her soft breasts pillowing the back of his neck. She cooed, "Oscar, I can't believe how you've grown! Your shoulders are so wide—so big and strong now!" He had rushed into the bathroom and jerked off with excitement. After that embarrassing episode, Oscar began to avoid Cleo. His guilt was worsened by his parent's constant reference to Cleo as "your big sister," so he was glad he was leaving for Atlanta the next morning.

CHAPTER NINE

IT DESCENDED ON THE castle like the dust storms roaring across the plains, so dense one could see neither behind nor ahead. There was no time left to devise plans for saving the castle. The taxes that had been assessed were impossible to pay. Banks all over America and Europe closed.

Staff members moved in slow motion, backs bent like icy trees in winter. Brows were wrinkled like barren fields, and smiles twisted into grimaces in a matter of seconds. Simple greetings degenerated into moans. As a whole, they seemed lost in a ghostly shroud of defeat.

Those few remaining students shared a feeling that alien forces, both mysterious and terrible, had invaded their premises. The effect was that of an eerie presence, vague and annoying, floating in the air. There were obvious manifestations of trouble that could not be denied. New students were turned away even though there was more than enough room for them. More girls were mysteriously "farmed out" or disappeared without a good-bye.

It was a fall morning, clear and crisp, and breezes plucked blossoms from their cradles to perform a colorful dying dance. Cleo watched this display against the steely glaze of the sky with an unmistakable sense of life's futility. She had skipped breakfast, and since everything was in disarray, she was sure no one would care. Instead she went out for a walk in the gardens. The brisk wind on her face did nothing to dispel her mood of gloom and apprehension. Cleo walked in the direction of the springs, but the relentless uneasiness she felt continued, the cold wind adding to her feeling of discomfort. Cleo walked swiftly along a path bordered by fading roses, barely noticing their nodding blossoms.

A circular stone bench appeared before her, and she sat heavily down, surrounded by a multicolored bed of flowers in overripe, untamed profusion. The scent was almost nauseating—too sweet and too pungent—and reminded her of a funeral. Instantly, her thoughts turned to her own future, not how she would die, but how she would live: *What am I going to do when the castle closes? Where shall I go? What will become of me?* In this dark mood, she continued on, and her hand was pierced by thorny stems as she walked down the narrow path through the bushes.

Cleo stood sucking her bleeding finger and realized she was in too foul a mood to walk alone—she needed company or she might be tempted to jump into the lake. For a flash of a second, she saw herself, lying in the lake fully clothed, her body shimmering colorfully on its sandy bottom, bubbles floating upward toward the surface.

"This is too spooky," she said aloud, "I'm much too irritated to be alone." She would go back and find Edna and draw her into some diverting activity. Maybe they would rehearse their lines for *The Cat and the Whippoorwill,* the original play they had written together and would perform Friday night.

Cleo turned back toward the castle, head bowed, blown by the wind. When she rounded the building and approached the courtyard, she saw a luxurious, dark green car, its top down, with shiny leather seats. To her surprise, Edna was sitting in the car with a wealthy-looking, dark-skinned, attractive Negro couple.

Two of the castle girls were standing by the car waving, while another was near the back, caressing the canvas of the rolled-back top. She heard one of the students ask the driver what kind of car it was, and he replied in a proud tone, "Miss, this is a Cadillac, a four-passenger Sport Phaeton." The man was just about to start the engine as Cleo walked onto the courtyard terrace and stood directly in front of his car.

When Edna saw Cleo, she said something to the pretty lady sitting next to her, swiftly climbed out of the car, and came running toward her. Cleo felt a shock pierce like a needle through her body, paralyzing her so she couldn't move, even when Edna hugged her.

Edna said, cheerfully, "Cleo, I was looking all over for you. I'm going to be adopted. I just found out. They have to go back to Texas now, and they're taking me with them."

Cleo felt a flash of heat rise in her face. She wanted to cry but instead bit her lip and lifted her chin toward the breeze. They were all staring at her, and it was as if everything was frozen in time and space. Cleo could hear no sounds—she just watched the silent people hovering around the big, shiny car. Yet, in the next moment, the sound of voices returned, with the hum of the car's engine.

Cleo stood very straight and still. She thought, *Edna is leaving, and I'll never see her again.* Then the recriminations came: *Why didn't anyone tell me? They know how close we are.* Admittedly, there was so much the staff would never know: Many times, the two girls protected each other after a harsh criticism, a reprimand, or some other offense that sent one or the other to sulk in the castle's dark recesses, attempting to hide where there was no hiding place. Edna knew Cleo's dark moods as no others did and used her bubbly ways to cheer her up. And now she was leaving.

Cleo forced her paralyzed arms to lift from her sides and embrace Edna. She kissed her cheek, skin that felt soft and cool, while her own cheeks burned with shame. She was speechless with emotions that words could not express. Finally, she heard herself say, "I'm so happy for you, Edna. Have a wonderful time with your new family."

Edna squeezed her hands and said, "I love you, Cleo, my dear, dear sister. I'll write as soon as I get to Texas."

And then, waving back at all the others, Edna ran and jumped into the car, and they were off, a flurry of good-byes ringing out behind them, their chatter sounding like bells on goats run amok. Some of the girls rushed after the car until its wheels crushed on the hard gravel, rounded the corner, and turned onto the dusty road. Cleo could not move from where she stood but lifted an arm in a dispirited gesture just as the car disappeared from view. And that was the last time she heard from her friend.

CHAPTER TEN

OSCAR RETURNED FROM ATLANTA University three years later, taller than before, his voice even deeper and his lanky body more filled out. Returning to the small, lifeless town was hard for him after the noisy stimulation of Atlanta. Before he entered college, he had been content to hibernate on his visits home, reading books, playing ball with friends on the old Normal School's abandoned playground, or playing his sax on the back steps. But now he felt not only apathy but also a sense of dissociation.

Oscar decided to take Mrs. Redd up on her offer to read any book he wanted in her extensive home library. She had said, "Oscar, just knock on the door, and if I'm not home, walk right in, take a book and sit yourself down in a comfortable chair in my study, and read. There's always milk in the icebox and you know where the cookie jar is." People in Springhill's close-knit neighborhood did not lock their doors. That would have been an affront to neighbors who were in and out of each other's houses, borrowing books and bringing pies, jars of homemade preserves, and other shared items.

Oscar followed Mrs. Redd's invitation, wandered into the kitchen, and discovered some chocolate chip cookies. He made a snack, poured a glass of cold milk, and returned to her study. He browsed through her volumes and found an interesting looking set of books. He spent the next hours reading about A. C. Treadwell's life, his travels out West, and how he met Isaac Naylor, the giant.

Oscar wondered why sane men with lots of money would come back to this town after having experienced the adventures of the far West. Treadwell's descriptions appeared to be unbelievably exciting. Oscar wished he could leave the South and visit the places that Treadwell had described. Oscar had never in his life seen "snow-capped mountains" or "green valleys stretched in a panorama of magical colors as far as the eyes could see," as Treadwell's chronicles depicted. Oscar longed for something more than what existed here in this little town, with its dead fields and broken-down shacks, dilapidated houses streaked with peeling paint, and the constant red dust rising from the dirt roads. He could see Springhill dying right before his eyes. He could feel the devastation of the people, doing little more than hanging on, waiting for things to get better—or worse.

One Sunday morning, Oscar walked up the hill to the castle. After reading Treadwell's book, he was looking forward to meeting Isaac Naylor. He had told his father about his plans, to which Albert responded, "Son, go anywhere you like." This freedom, a reward for his college student status, was responsible for his renewed enthusiasm and his fast sprint up the steep hill.

But even though he had been told that the castle was closed, the shock of its state of dilapidation stunned him. It was impossible to see inside, for the building was completely boarded up. He stood dumbfounded as he imagined the collapse of its interior as well, vacant rooms with rattraps placed all around its perimeters—in cellars, attics, halls, and kitchen pantries. As he walked on, he noticed several bungalows that were also in need of paint and structural repair, although he understood that some families still lived in them. Mrs. King and her daughter, Stacey, had moved to Chicago, where Alice had an important job as head of the business school at Chicago University, and Stacey was studying at the Chicago Art Institute.

Oscar walked on, but as he glanced back at the dismal sight of the castle, it evoked a sense of forlorn despair, casting a pall over everything—as if signaling the end of life was imminent. Oscar treaded deeper into the quiet woods, his boots crunching on dried leaves, the dead tree limbs underfoot alternating with new green growths visible here and there. When he came upon the springs, he realized he had taken an unexpected turn. The glistening water seemed to move in a rhythm that was almost like a beckoning gesture. He thought of how good it would feel to take a swim in the cool, clear water and wash away the stifling grit that seemed to be closing his pores and eating away the good feelings of freedom he had experienced when he began his walk.

One of the reasons he wanted to come here was to check out the castle as a place where his best friends from college could hang out when they came for a visit at the end of June. "Ha!" he said aloud as he thought how they would laugh at him for bragging about the beautiful castle where his jazz trio had been the headliner. This place would be really disappointing, especially for Emmett Lansing, who lived in a mansion in Harlem and would be visiting him for the first time. He had heard from others that Emmett's house was beautiful and that he had photographs proving that he had actually gone with his father to poetry-reading teas at Alain Locke's home. Now Oscar cursed himself for inviting his friends to this dump.

He came to an unexpected clearing and was instantly overwhelmed by a gold-colored dome rising above the pine trees. Excited now that he'd found the home of the legendary giant, Oscar stood very still, wondering if he should go farther. He had heard that the giant was a hermit, completely estranged from the world, and never left his house. However, Treadwell's writings described him as a good and noble man. This gave him the courage to continue his journey. As Oscar entered the clearing, he saw him—a gigantic Negro with great muscled arms poised above his head that caused Oscar to take a deep breath before walking slowly forward just as the giant plunged his ax into a log with incredible speed, splitting it.

Oscar had not expected Isaac to be so towering. But so many legends had grown up around the solitary giant who lived in the woods, he hadn't known what to expect. The stories were forever changing, but he felt reassured when he recalled from reading the book in Mrs. Redd's library that both Treadwell and the Indians had found him to be an honorable person.

Isaac Naylor suddenly looked in Oscar's direction. The giant left the ax imbedded in the log, wiped his face with a handkerchief, and quickly walked toward Oscar.

When Isaac reached him, Oscar stretched his neck backward and held his hand up, saying in a voice smaller than he would have liked, "Good afternoon, I'm Oscar, the Wallaces' boy." As Isaac took his hand, Oscar thought, *Why did I say that? Of all things, I called myself a* boy? As the giant held Oscar's small hand in his strong grasp and smiled down at him, Oscar added, "Uh, I mean, I'm Cordelia and Albert Wallace's son. How do you do?"

Isaac bent from his waist and said in a gentle but deep voice, "My name is Isaac. It's good to meet you, son." Then laughing, he added, "I already know who you are."

"Oh, have we met before?" Oscar shook his head and quickly added, "Ah, that's impossible. I would have remembered."

"No, we haven't met, but I know who you are, Oscar. I've known you for a long time. You go to college in Atlanta, where you are a very enlightened and notable student. And I hear you play a mean saxophone."

Oscar was astounded! He knew for a fact that Isaac had never been to their house—he probably couldn't even stand up in their house. "Mr. Isaac, I'm so glad to meet you, but how do you know these things about me?"

Isaac leaned forward, a friendly but playfully mocking smile spreading across his face, wrinkling a place underneath his eyes and sending his already slanted eyebrows upward toward his slicked-back, shiny black hair without a speck of gray. "I have spies, you see, who bring me only good news. I insist on only good news, and you are my prime source for the good. Call me Isaac."

Isaac suddenly stood straight up and, making an expansive gesture toward the house, said, "Come into my inner sanctuary. Perhaps we can continue this conversation over a couple of Coca-Colas." He was already lumbering down a path filled with white pebbles toward an open space bordered by azaleas.

Oscar followed, running to catch up with him, as they entered a stand of pines in whose center stood a very tall adobe house. It was built of stone and wood with colored glass panels around an upper ledge and door, topped off by the big gold dome that Oscar had first seen rising above the trees.

Oscar said, trying to seem blasé, "Quite a house, sir. Do you live here alone?"

"Drop the 'sir,' just call me Isaac. I live alone here, except for my friendly animals over yonder in the pasture." He made an expansive movement with his arms. "I'll take you there someday."

He led Oscar toward a large door with stained glass around its oval perimeter. "Come, let's go inside, and have a cold Coca-Cola."

Once inside, Oscar was astonished by the serenity and the peace of the room. A shifting light immediately drew his eyes upward. Through the dome's painted glass, Oscar could see the sky here and there but asked himself if the color was just a heavenly blue painted on the glass ceiling to resemble an almost cloudless sky.

"Did you build this magnificent place yourself?" Oscar asked, and turned to Isaac who was observing him—not looking—but observing him in an intense way. For a moment Oscar was afraid, but only for a moment.

"I'll go get those Coca-Colas," Isaac said as he walked into another room. Shortly, he returned holding two frosted Coke bottles in one huge hand. "Come over here. We can see all the colors of the universe from this angle." He led Oscar to a rug with an eagle woven in its center. When he looked upward, he saw the prism, fielding its universal colors in shifting rays around the room.

Oscar was struck by the design of the adobe—the light, the colors, the stone and brick. Wishing to know everything at once, Oscar's questions came in inquisitive spurts.

Isaac explained, "I lived out West for a while and built this as an adobe house, although the clay/soil mixture is different here from that in the West. So I experimented. This hillside is full of minerals and red clay. My helpers mined the clay and baked it a long time during the dry seasons. We had to reinforce everything with this stone to protect it against moisture. It's more humid here in Georgia than in the Southwest. Unfortunately, we went through an extended drought at one time—bad for the farms—but it helped the construction."

"This light ... it comes like a rainbow from those windows and just invades this space like the light in a cathedral. I've never seen anything like it!" Oscar gazed about the room with an expression of wonder.

Isaac said, "I dreamed this light." He paused, and then Oscar laughed. Isaac continued, "No, Oscar, don't laugh, for it's true. The masters of Chartres, twelfth-century architects, saw visions that resulted in the building of cathedrals in harmony with God and the universe. They didn't really know what the results would be until it was done."

Oscar remembered his mother and father talking about the giant, and they mentioned that he was not an educated man. Yet, there was this talk of architecture, and there were books on shelves all along the curved walls from the glazed and polished stone seat, upward to a kind of loft, which circled the entire room. The shelves were lined with books by authors like Walt Whitman, Robert Frost, and even Booker T. Washington. Oscar walked around, peering at other books—Plato, Shakespeare, Proust, Sartre, Kafka, and Homer's *The Odyssey.*

"Have you read all these books?" Oscar asked.

"Most," Isaac said. "What I like best is reading them aloud to myself. That way one never forgets the words. And I must admit, I've had plenty of time, being somewhat of a loner. At least, until now."

Under the glow of the constantly changing rays of light, Oscar and Isaac talked about his life at Atlanta University and discussed their favorite books.

Oscar told Isaac about A. C. Treadwell's writings in Mrs. Redd's library, which told how he met up with Isaac out West.

Isaac appeared baffled by Oscar's revelation, asking, "What was it that you read in Mrs. Redd's library?"

Oscar repeated that they were Treadwell's chronicles of his explorations and included his discovery of gold with Isaac as his fellow prospector.

"I knew A. C. ended each day by writing," Isaac said, "but I was never sure exactly what it was he wrote."

Oscar told Isaac that he was the hero of A. C.'s chronicles.

Isaac said, "When we first met out there in the wilds, I was with a band of Indians who had adopted me. But after we talked over a wonderful feast he had prepared for us, we all felt comfortable. Oscar, when men are out there all alone, the stars seem close and fiery above the silent woods, so vivid that you believe they already know all your secrets, and in such circumstances men bond easily with each other. Even though I loved my adopted Indian family, finding A. C. was like discovering a long-lost brother.

"Together, A. C. and I outsmarted an Army regiment that was hell-bent on wiping out the Indians. We planned our escape on the first night we met, while we did guard duty around his campfire. So naturally, we discussed our life experiences and discovered we had much in common. Both of us had run away from home because we were victims of our parents' overzealous religious beliefs.

"I was born in Buffalo, New York, and at the age of thirteen I inadvertently brought shame on my entire family—both schoolteachers and devout Jehovah's Witnesses. My father was an elder in the church and noted for his oratorical skills. I evidently inherited these traits. Beginning at the age of seven, I preached the Gospel of hell and heaven while distributing *The Watchtower* door-to-door in unfamiliar neighborhoods. When I was thirteen, after years of speaking eloquently, my voice was silenced. I will never forget the day or the moment this happened.

"My cohorts and I called upon an elderly farm couple—friendly, warm, and welcoming—but in the moment I opened my mouth to speak, only gasps and squeaks spewed from my throat. I could not utter a word. After weeks, during which many types of spiritual and medicinal cures were administered, to no avail, the elders concluded that my condition was the work of the devil. They subjected me to a procedure called 'shunning.' Although everyone was to treat me kindly, no one could speak to me ... not even my family, until there was a specific sign that I had returned to the graces of God.

"During this period of isolation, perpetual prayers for my recovery resounded in my ears. There was this everlasting chant going on for my salvation. One night a violent spirit must have taken over my being and burst through in the form of obscene writings that covered my bedroom walls. To this day, I do not know where the words came from; they were not in my vocabulary. To release my parents from pain, I left home with a small bag of food and a change of clothes and faced alone the dark cold of the night. I was thirteen years old and over six feet tall, weighing in at about one hundred and eighty pounds. My great size turned out to be a blessing, for immediately I found steady work with crews building the railroads, and worked my way westward. Later, I decided to set off on my own and explore the fantastically beautiful regions of the West, and there I met my Indian friends, who seemed at first to think I was a chief of mythological renown who had finally returned to them from ancient times.

"As I said, there are similarities in both A. C.'s and my childhood experiences. A. C. got his initials instead of a name because he was believed to be 'the second coming of Christ' by his adoptive parents, who discovered him in a manger in their barn. They named him 'A. C.,' meaning 'After Christ.' Treadwell told me that he was an object of extreme worship and devotion; his church held yearly revival meetings with him playing the part of Christ. He ran away from home at the age of twelve to escape the disdain of his two older adoptive brothers, who had been neglected because of him, and the harassment of his schoolmates. Most of them knew the true story of A. C.'s mother and father's drunken binges; she gave birth in the barn in her usual alcoholic stupor, and they all knew of her subsequent demise shortly after A. C.'s birth. So, you see what I mean when I say we had a lot in common. During our explorations, we developed a reverence for the earth's natural resources and respect for mankind and the universe. When Treadwell and I came here, it was our goal to live in peace and harmony with man and nature. I suspect you know some of these events from reading Treadwell's diary."

Oscar said, "No, I didn't see anything about his childhood or yours in the pages I read."

"Well, we may be the only humans who learned the whole truth about each other," Isaac responded with a sad face.

Oscar blurted out, "This is the most wonderful place I have ever seen! May I bring my friends from college here to meet you? They'll be so awed by your books. I work at the library at college, and you have more great books than they have. Where did you get all these books?" His words rushed on without having gotten an answer to his first question.

"I ordered most of them from book dealers in Boston and New York."

Oscar could say only, "That's cool," imitating the lingo of the jazz musicians he often tried to emulate.

They continued talking through an afternoon shower that pounded against the windows, and Oscar wished he had the artistic ability to paint the scene, or at least embed the images deeply in his mind so he would never forget it.

"You can bring your buddies on one condition. Don't tell anyone else except your parents. And, if it doesn't work out, you can count on me being the first to tell you so … and you must keep a promise to leave if that happens."

"Thank you so much. I feel so honored. Thanks."

"I'll let you know after each visit if you can come again. But, to tell you the truth, Oscar, lately I feel in need of human company, especially the company of an intelligent person like you."

Oscar wanted to hug him but decided that would be dumb, so he looked up at Isaac and said gravely, "Thank you, Isaac, you can count on me to uphold your rules. How do I let you know we're coming?"

"Just come on a Saturday or Sunday, in the afternoon. I'll be expecting you whenever you and your friends decide to come."

Oscar got up to leave; Isaac opened the door with the leaded glass windows along its sides. It was late in the afternoon, yet there was so much light in the house. Oscar looked around once more, declaring, "This light, it's amazing. This place should be one of the wonders of the world!" After thanking Isaac again, he took off running. He couldn't wait to bring his friends to meet Isaac and talk with him about his books. He thought, *How phenomenal it is to have someone like Isaac, right here in this little town.*

Oscar could hardly endure the next few weeks in Atlanta, even though he loved the campus and the activities there. He was a very popular young man on campus, admired for his many skills. He was a fine musician, known especially for his saxophone melodies—regularly propelling the girls across the lawns to the boys' dorms to listen to the music in rapturous trances.

Oscar invited his friends to the giant's adobe, and they were eager to leave campus for an exciting weekend.

Audrey Durant, a plump, sweet-faced, dimpled beauty and Springhill native, was a first-year student at Spelman College in Atlanta. Audrey and Ophelia were great friends, and they decided to take the train together from Atlanta to Springhill. Oscar had also invited his friends, Matthew—a piano prodigy from Tennessee—and Emmett Lansing. Emmett had traveled widely in the United States, Africa, and Europe with his father, the publisher of *Harlem Voices*, a popular newspaper that presented new works from elite writers of the Harlem Renaissance.

Cordelia welcomed Oscar and his friends. She picked vegetables from her gardens and directed her husband to take the chicken and meats that had been marinating for some time out to the barbecue pit that had been dug in the fields of the now vacant Springhill Normal School next door. But Cordelia was surprised when Oscar informed her that he, Emmett, Matthew, Audrey, Cleo, and Ophelia would be going to a barbecue at Isaac's place the next Sunday afternoon. Because she knew so little about Isaac, Cordelia was somewhat apprehensive that her children and their friends would be visiting his home. However, she took comfort in the fact that they were going together as a group. She was also pleased that in preparation for their day with Isaac, they spent hours each evening reading books, writing poetry, and singing hymns. Cordelia had heard Oscar admonish Ophelia, who had fallen back into the habit of reading romantic novels, to turn to philosophy instead. Cordelia was pleased to note that Oscar had bought Ophelia a volume of poetry by Phillis Wheatley—poems on various religious and moral subjects.

Sunday was a warm day as the group—Oscar, Audrey, Ophelia, Emmett, and Matthew—stood under the chinaberry tree in the front yard waiting for Cleo to join them.

Since the castle had been forced to close its doors, Cleo had been living at the Redds' home—in a studio apartment her dance teacher, Gwen, had fashioned in her mother's house. Gwen had since moved to New York City, and they were all excited about her coveted role in Katherine Dunham's dance company, now performing *Emperor Jones*.

Cleo had been seventeen when the last of the students at the castle were relocated. A part of her wished she could stay inside the crumbling walls, like some of those old women one reads about, whose houses are covered in spider webs and finally fall in on their heads. But she knew that was not possible.

As for going to college, she was tired of living with groups of girls and teachers. It would be a continuation of her past—rules, schedules, and strangers encroaching on her space. She had given much thought to the Wallaces' generous invitation to come and live with them, but though she loved the family and felt forever in their debt, Cleo craved the privacy she'd never had.

The Wallaces respected both Cleo's need for privacy and her decision to take a year off before going to college. The couple helped her secure a job as a receptionist at Springhill Memorial, the hospital Albert had founded.

Cleo had never lived outside institution walls, and now, alone in the studio, Cleo felt like a grown-up at last, living in her own apartment, with a job she loved.

She was in high spirits when the young people met at the Wallace home a week later for their visit to the giant's adobe.

It was a bright Sunday in June, even though a large gray cloud on the western horizon signaled the possibility of rain. Oscar held Audrey's hand while pointing out various birds, trees, and plants. As they left the road and started up the steep red hill into the pine forest, they heard the noisy sounds of a flock of chickadees that swooped downward, barely missing their heads. They ducked and ran, laughing about being attacked by a flock of birds. But then, just past a grove of oaks, they were sobered by the sight of the castle appearing above them, and stood in solemn disbelief, for its beauty was still prevalent despite the boarded-up windows. Its façade was made more presentable by the vines, festooned with large white flowers, which covered its walls, as if attempting to hide its lost soul.

They walked the five or so miles through the pines to the other side of the woods. Along the way, the girls picked violets, daisies, dogwood, and honeysuckle. Cleo, Audrey, and Ophelia wore colorful cotton sundresses, whose vivid patterns almost duplicated the flowers they held in their arms.

Just as the sun rose to its midday zenith, the adobe's crown flashed above the treetops. More animated, they walked swiftly despite the sun's powerful rays beating down on them.

Then they saw him. Isaac stood out in a cleared part of his yard just past the meadow grass, bent over, shirtless, intent on tidying the cleared space. Even though Oscar and Cleo had seen Isaac before, they were as awed as the others.

Isaac stepped forward, smiling broadly. "Welcome! Just give me a moment to correct my state of undress." His wonderful voice sounded as if it resonated somewhere deep inside before pouring soothingly from his lips. The sunlight accented his muscular arms, glistening with perspiration, as he pulled his shirt on.

Isaac's size was at first startling, and Oscar noted a flicker of fear in his companions' eyes. But Isaac was so genuinely kind and comforting, the instant of uncertainty passed quickly.

Isaac was effusive in his greetings, shaking each visitor's hand, and repeating, "It's so good to have you! Welcome to my home."

As they entered the house through the massive double doors, the group expressed its enchantment on first sight with "Oh's" and "Ah's." The visitors turned around and around, pointing to various artifacts, their admiring gestures and comments leading to questions. Most came up with answers to explain the architectural quintessence as if they knew what they were talking about.

Out of this babble of voices emerged several informed opinions. Emmett said with a great deal of verve, "One is immediately transformed in an ethereal way, as if in a gothic cathedral." Cleo said as if in a trance, "There is such a balance between light, form, and color." Matthew said poetically, "This round room promotes peaceful continuity, as circular spaces are known to bring about a sense of calm connection."

Isaac directed them to the stone bench that followed the round contours of the room, its seats hollowed out. They all stood mute, questions in their eyes, before they finally sat.

Emmett asked, "How did you build this stone bench so that it follows the roundness of the walls? It's a bit like the pictures of stone troughs for cattle I've seen in my research of ancient Egypt. How did you put it together and carve seats in it like this?"

Isaac explained that the benches were indeed animal feeding troughs made of stone that had been cleaned and polished and selected for their fit to the whole. Along the backs of the benches and all about the room were pillows covered with brightly colored fabrics of Native American designs. The room's floor was polished stone that resembled marble.

Oscar asked Isaac to tell them about the colorful, symmetrical patterns reflected on the walls.

Isaac explained that the prism was made from a number of geometrically aligned panels with planes of various shapes and colors set in abstract patterns. Three glass panels, floating silently above them, were similar to elongated chimes, picking up the light of colored glass as the sunlight filtered through them, reflecting on the walls the prismatic images of the universe.

The noon sun wove unique patterns on the walls of the adobe, and everyone sat as if in a hypnotic trance. Then, as if moved by a sudden wave of awareness, they began asking questions in quick succession. Oscar asked, "What stories are being told by the designs on the stained glass?"

Isaac said, "The designs came to me in a dream, and when I awakened, I drew them as they had appeared. Later I discovered they almost duplicated designs from ancient Aztec cave drawings."

Audrey, straining her head upward, said to him, "The stained glass windows seem to tell the stories of rituals that loom up out of the collective consciousness of many cultures."

Isaac, smiling, walked over to Audrey and took her hand, leading her outside. "You are absolutely right. Come, I'll show you!"

Soon they were all outside, and Isaac was squatting in the clearing, with the group circled around him, drawing designs with a large stick and explaining the various rituals that were depicted in each.

Later, they roasted loads of fresh peanuts, eating them hot off the grill, accompanied by frosted Coca-Colas. They went inside to escape the heat of the hot sun and ate fresh vegetable salad, barbecued chicken, corn on the cob, greens, apple pie, and finally coffee from a metal camp pitcher. As they sat, conversing leisurely, a sense of camaraderie wrapped them all in its comforting embrace.

Isaac invited everyone to look through his library and pick a book to read or recite, while he fetched wood for the fire, in case it should rain. He looked smaller going through the door, wide enough for two normal persons to exit together.

They all browsed along the circular walls for a favorite book. Matthew was thrilled to find a book about the Jubilee Singers of Fisk University, where he was studying, that contained news about their recent travels and awards.

Cleo found a libretto of the Broadway musical, *Shuffle Along*, and was singing softly "Love Will Find a Way."

Oscar was still searching, as were Audrey and Ophelia, when Isaac returned with a huge armload of wood and said, "The weather is really nice now. Before we settle down for our readings, how about a tour of the grounds? I'll show you my farmlands."

Isaac gestured for them to follow, and as they passed, he pointed to a door marked with a large painting of a willow and said, "Here is the inside toilet, and there are several outside toilet sheds all over the property; make your choice as needed. Grab a Coca-Cola, if you like, to take with you."

They opened their bottles on the wall brackets and followed Isaac into a narrow hallway. Isaac pushed against a bookcase panel, knocking three times, and it opened to reveal some descending stairs. He called, "Follow me!"

The stairs led to an underground cavern. The floor was covered with old stones with a glossy sealant. They walked ahead for about thirty feet, and at the end was an arch with heavy doors; Isaac pushed open the doors and led them down seven more steps into a small, secluded garden. As they looked back from whence they came, they noticed vines completely obscured the door so that from the outside, the door was completely hidden from view.

Isaac told them to look upward, where there was an opening in the leaf-covered arbor, through which the sun's rays beamed down on various statuary in a circle along the edges of the garden.

"This is where I come each dawn to meditate. This compass, directly under the arbor's opening, will soon be completed. I'm working on small statuaries that will be placed on the compass top to indicate hours of the day.

"There is an underground passage from here to the stables. All you have to do is press that button and the passage opens. Keeps you dry all the way to the end of the property in case of bad weather." Isaac pointed toward the stables in the distance.

"Come dressed for horseback and hay rides on your next visit. The sun will be setting soon, so we had better get back to the house."

Once they were back inside, though the house was still bright with magical light, Isaac said, "It's late now, and I wonder if you would come next week, prepared with either your own creative ideas and writings, or your favorite works from the books you've borrowed."

They departed as the sun was starting its rapid descent, its light filtering through the pine trees, illuminating their path homeward out of the forest. Several large oaks at the edge of the forest formed a mammoth chapel adorned with points of sunlight. Beyond them, they could see the sun sinking on the horizon. The sudden glare, the dustiness, and its intrusion caused them to gasp in unison. Oscar said, "It's such a shock to return to the real world."

CHAPTER ELEVEN

D R. JIMMY BLANCHARD HAD many reasons to be grateful for Albert Wallace's vision. Before Wallace chose him to head a hospital in Springhill, Dr. Blanchard had never considered working in the United States. Fortunately, he saw Wallace's advertisement in the *Advocate*, a liberal Barbadian newspaper. The job opening was for a physician to head a new hospital in Springhill, Georgia, and it had come at a most opportune time for Blanchard. Barbados was still reeling from the bloody riots that had been spurred by a severe economic crisis. Jimmy seized upon the opportunity to leave Barbados; the climate was temperate, the monetary offer was exceptional, and he could avoid the political chaos swirling around his father, one of the leaders of the Independent Labor party, who was considered a dangerous radical by the ruling classes and a benevolent savior by the poor.

Another reason for Jimmy to come to the United States was that his sister, Hattie, had resided in Chicago for several years, and on many occasions she had invited Jimmy to come live with her. Dr. Blanchard preferred to practice in Great Britain, where he had completed his medical studies. However, his father's political affiliations would probably hinder his opportunity to achieve a successful position there.

When Dr. Blanchard and the other recruited physicians met with Albert Wallace in Barbados, they had all been impressed with this educated American Negro who held the position of college president and was also acclaimed for his work as a mathematician and inventor.

Dr. Jimmy Blanchard was hired as the administrator of the new hospital, as well as its chief surgeon. Dr. Blanchard initially had some misgivings about going to work in the southern part of the United States after learning the races were completely segregated and Negroes were even forbidden treatment at local hospitals. Albert told the doctors during their first meeting that he had watched helplessly as his wife suffered and almost died while delivering their third child. To his credit, he had insisted that Cordelia be saved even if that meant the death of the baby.

After losing the baby during birth, Albert worked tirelessly with the town's leaders—black and white—to build a Negro hospital. He finally succeeded in convincing the town's white leaders to put up the money to rehabilitate an abandoned property that had once housed a white nursing home. Many of the town's Negro artisans volunteered their services to rehabilitate the building, which became Springhill Memorial Hospital for Negroes, a modern, licensed medical facility. Three other West Indian physicians came with Dr. Blanchard.

The doctors were treated to the best that southern, colored hospitality could offer. The generous and thankful "Mamas" of Springhill provided loving care, spicy barbecues, and Sunday dinners that increased the girth of at least two of the doctors. But this was not the case with Jimmy Blanchard. The energy he radiated from without must have been moving around within, for he remained slim and tall, with the same athletic build he brought with him from the soccer fields of Barbados.

When Albert first examined the resumes of the doctors he had chosen, he could see that Dr. Blanchard stood out from the rest. He was self-assured yet modest, studious yet personable, introspective yet outgoing. His medical studies had been completed in Great Britain; he received highest honors from Cambridge College and Edinburgh

University Medical School. Yet, he was naturally personable and open, unpretentious and charismatic.

At Cordelia's urging, Cleo had taken business courses at Springhill Normal. She excelled in her typing, shorthand, and accounting. Cleo was given the dual jobs of receptionist and secretary to Dr. Blanchard. The Wallaces offered her this position after Cleo made clear to her benefactors that she wanted to work instead of entering college.

Cleo was a fast learner and was respected by the staff as well as those patients with whom she had occasional contact. She loved her work and felt at last she had found her niche in life. Dr. Jimmy Blanchard and Cleo had been working closely together for several months, and from the beginning there was a great chemistry between them.

Cleo had already decided any personal relationship with Dr. Blanchard was out of the question. His home was in Barbados, and she certainly had no intention of going there. She knew she attracted his attention, but she was determined to maintain a friendly working relationship. Dr. Blanchard seemed to her a gentleman, and he had treated her with respect.

Dr. Blanchard assigned Cleo to a small office directly off his larger office, and her space also opened into the reception hall. Cleo felt this arrangement was not at all by accident, for there was a larger office across the hall near the nurse's station and the entrance to the hospital, which appeared to her more suitable for her duties as a receptionist. She noticed with some uneasiness the "accidental" brushes of his hand on her back in passing and his habit of standing unnecessarily close to her when they were discussing business. However, so far, he had done nothing particularly inappropriate.

Cleo knew that many thought Dr. Blanchard a ladies' man, but he treated her politely and with friendly decorum, and she wanted to keep it that way. She did not believe those rumors of his association with street women, because he was unusually immaculate, from his well-groomed hair and clean-shaven face, down to his polished shoes. She certainly knew better than to get involved in questionable liaisons;

that much she had learned from the staff at the castle, who brought the girls up to be ladies.

Yet, Cleo was flattered by the doctor's attention. After all, he was handsome, hard working, and smart. As chief of the hospital and a surgeon, he had the best job in town.

Another characteristic that had been ingrained in the girls during their years at the castle had been to plan ahead and keep their eyes on their goals. Cleo could still hear clearly in her head Alice King's admonitions, "Let no man distract you from your first duty, and that is to yourself. Here at the castle, we teach you how to achieve success on your own terms without your being dependent on a man."

One Saturday morning, Dr. Blanchard telephoned her at her home and asked if he could drop off a proposal that needed immediate corrections because it had to be submitted to contractors the following Monday morning. Cleo's small apartment had a back entrance that separated it from the rest of the Redds' house. Cleo gave Blanchard directions to park his car in the backyard driveway. Hearing his knock, she opened the door and led him through the vestibule and into a small room furnished with a desk, typewriter, and two comfortable chairs. They went over the draft together, with Cleo penciling in the changes she would later type. When the task was completed, he pulled her chair back from her desk and she stood up.

Suddenly, and without uttering a word, he whirled her around to face him and encircled her waist with his hard, muscular arms, lifting her off her feet.

"What are you doing?" Cleo exclaimed.

"Something I've wanted to do from the first time I laid eyes on you, Cleo. I just can't be near you without wanting to hold you in my arms."

Jimmy pulled Cleo closer, kissing her cheeks, lips, and neck, pulling her hard against him, until her warmth matched his hunger and she no longer struggled against him. He held her fast in his arms, and in one motion pushed the chair aside, lifting her body upward as if she were weightless, placing her before him on top of the desk without resistance or struggle on her part whatsoever. She felt both mesmerized and defenseless as she allowed him—unbelievably—to kiss her neck and her throat, and unbutton her blouse. As he caressed her breasts, she said and did nothing except sigh loudly as a surge of unexpected passion poured forth from her. She felt like a bird, finally freed—wings beating a frantic rhythm, fighting to stay aloft.

Cleo was unprepared for the vibrations that chilled her spine yet warmed her skin, leaving her entire body throbbing with pain and pleasure. She feared she would swoon, become lost in him, his skin hers. He held his hand hard against her throbbing vulva, still covered by cotton panties. He held her for what seemed an eternity as he kissed her upturned face and throat, releasing a wetness that rushed through her, beyond her control to understand or terminate.

The only words she could articulate were "Stop, stop!" Yet, she found her arms locked around him, and she no longer possessed the will to stop him as his warm hands moved in rapid currents against her. Her limp and lifeless efforts to remove his hands from her buttocks failed to contain him. He lifted her as if she were made of soft down, spineless and open. Finally, her body faded into his, she moved in rhythm with his motions, breathing, sighing, and moaning with his moans. She clutched his body, longing to stay in this soft wet space, wishing never to be alone again. She clung to him, giving in to his deep kisses, feeling the urgency of his member against her thigh.

She did not care what would happen, or what she would do. She knew only that she wanted him, that he could do with her whatever he wished. And as her skin was set upon like needles across its surface, she sensed her body needed his to survive.

It had happened so quickly! He had not given her the time to think, to reflect; he had robbed her of the opportunity to act against his passionate advances. And now just as quickly, he moved his hands away from her body—those hot hands that had stayed there so long, warming her and holding firm. Now he was calmly smoothing her hair, buttoning her blouse, lifting her from the desktop, and placing her feet squarely on the floor.

Without saying a word, he looked lovingly into her eyes, a smile of victory forming on his lips. He kissed her forehead and stroked her dark curls with his hands, massaging her head gently with his fingertips, softly placing kisses on her hot cheeks.

Cleo tried to still the clamor within her body. She looked quizzically into his eyes as she fought back tears, and then buried her head in his chest, his starched shirt scratching her burning cheeks. She wanted to stay there against him forever.

"Cleo, I have to go now," he was saying. "Cleo, I have to go now," he said again as he pulled slowly away.

He spoke as if nothing had happened between them. "I need to get back to work. Thanks for helping me with the proposal. I appreciate your help so much. I'll see you on Monday."

And then, as though nothing had happened between them, he was gone. The door had shut. Cleo heard his car rolling slowly down the driveway and out onto the street. Cleo whispered, "He left, just like that; he came, he teased me, and he left." Stunned and embarrassed, angry and furious, she ran to her bedroom and threw herself onto the bed, crying out, "The bastard, who does he think he is?" She lay for a long time feeling bewildered, exhausted, and overcome with shame.

Cleo found it difficult to go through her paces that Saturday afternoon with her young dance students. Usually encouraging and kind, she felt irritable and impatient with them. "You girls are undisciplined! You will never become dancers and achieve your goals unless you work harder! I will not allow any more of this shoddy shuffling! Shape up or ship out!"

Her students glanced at one another, glared at Cleo, and rolled their eyes.

After her afternoon classes were completed, Cleo went to bed with a debilitating headache. She slept through the supper hour and then went about the apartment, pulling the shades down, locking all the windows and the doors. Even after she had secured the house, she remained fearful and afraid; weak and vulnerable.

Cleo lay in her bed on her back, staring at the ceiling and planning her revenge. "How dare he treat me like a whore! He wouldn't think of doing such a thing to any decent girl. It's because I have no family and no protection, just like Cordelia told me." Cleo thought of all the things she would do and say to him: "I'll resign my job and leave town! But first I'll walk in and slap him in the face!" She cried herself to sleep, without dreams or nightmares. But the morning sun brought its bright, fierce sunlight into her room, and a strong sense of resolve passed through her body like a steel beam, cold and firm.

CHAPTER TWELVE

B Y MONDAY MORNING, CLEO had completely regained her usual coolness and composure. She chose a white silk blouse buttoned high, covering much of her long neck, a light blue cotton suit with a fitted jacket, and a flared skirt that fell below her knees. She pinned her hair up in a severe bun, securing straying curls with several hairpins.

She looked in the round mirror above her vanity and was pleased with her businesslike appearance—the perfect outfit that bespoke breeding and class. She felt poised and stable, completely in charge of her emotions and ready to start her life anew. She promised herself she would never again lose control with Jimmy Blanchard. He was her employer, and that was it. She was there to work, and work she would.

"Why let him ruin my life when I have everything going for me? I am not giving up a good job because of him. I'll save my money like Gwen suggested, leave this stupid town, and join her dance group in New York." She felt resolute as she repeated these vows while walking the short distance to Springhill Memorial Hospital, hoping Saturday's debacle would fade from existence like a forgotten dream.

Cleo decided to bypass Dr. Blanchard's office—and her usual routine of checking his mail—and walked instead down the hall past the nurses' station. As she said good mornings all around, the nurses returned her greetings happily, but with questioning expressions written all over their faces. Cleo thought, *Is that just my imagination?*

When she entered her office, she was surprised to see an enormous bouquet of roses—two or three dozen—on her desk. She approached them gingerly as if something dangerous lurked inside their ostentatious beauty. She suddenly looked around, as though for a culprit, and found the nurses, Ellen and Tamara, peeking in. Cleo ignored them for the moment and reached for the card tied with a ribbon on a thorny stem.

Cleo read the card in silence and then turned to the nurses, shrugging her shoulders.

Ellen said, "We had no idea it was your birthday."

Tamara added, "How about going out to lunch with us to celebrate? We can all go to that li'l sandwich place on River Street."

Cleo hugged them and agreed, thinking that would be a good way to escape Dr. Blanchard's further attention. She had never known when her real birthday was but had selected one at the castle, along with all the other children who had no such knowledge. But the birthday she had selected was not this date.

As soon as the nurses returned to their duties, Cleo took off her jacket, hung it neatly on a hanger on the cloak rack, smoothed her demure, businesslike attire, and opened the sealed envelope with "Personal" written on it that was hidden in the flowers. Inside was a second card engraved with Dr. Blanchard's initials and written in his handwriting:

> *May I have the honor of your company to celebrate your birthday, April 30, for dinner at the Chicken Shack, 40 River Street. Dinner will be served promptly at 6:00 PM.*
> *A car will come for you at 5:30 PM.*
> *Jimmy Blanchard.*

At that moment, members of the nursing staff were gathered in a little group on the second floor, agreeing that they were not surprised at all that Dr. Blanchard had finally, after all these months, made his move. They had noticed a recent change in his attitude. Dr. Blanchard was a hard taskmaster, running the hospital authoritatively, not giving the nurses and staff much slack. But if they wanted to soften him up, all they had to do was approach him when Cleo was in the room. He seemed a different man when she was around—more benevolent and affable. Yet, in all their secret talks, the personnel at the hospital looked upon this budding, romantic relationship with a great deal of skepticism, and all agreed that if Dr. Blanchard and Cleo entered into a romantic liaison, it would be a disaster.

Cleo had been protected all her life, at least from the time she came to the castle at the age of seven. In fact, Jimmy was the first man she had ever kissed.

Cleo was the doctor's counterpart as far as vitality and good looks were concerned, but her personality was decidedly the opposite. Cleo seemed to most people to maintain an aloof, formal presence—distant and reserved. But those who were lucky enough to know her well received in return kindness, warmth, and loyal friendship. The protective armor she had worn to get through this past weekend was the same she had used most of her life—denial, fantasy, and determination.

She also had a dramatic, charismatic presence. Tall and willowy, with a slim swan's neck and a ballet dancer's posture, her total image was out of place in Springhill, a poor, southern farming community. Her uniqueness led many to accuse her incorrectly of putting on airs or being unfriendly.

Cleo sensed that she existed in a lonely sphere—a world apart from others. She agreed with her detractors: How could anyone trust a woman whose beginnings are lost—hidden from not only others but herself as well? She very much wanted to be accepted and appreciated by other women, but she remained unsure of herself, inwardly, and her relationship so far with Jimmy Blanchard had not improved her self-image.

Dr. Blanchard usually insisted on an open-door policy between his office and Cleo's. But today she had closed that door, and her head was bent low over a ledger, pen in hand, when the connecting door swung open.

She was startled by his tall figure casting a shadow over her desk, as he strode quickly into the room. He did not ask if he might talk with her, or ask some question about the hospital, or if he might have a meeting with her.

He came in resolutely and stood behind her desk, bending over her as if examining the ledger on her desk, moving closer to her than he needed to be.

When Cleo lifted her head, she saw he was looking roguishly at her.

"Tell me," he said, "what would hold your attention so earnestly after I enter your office? Let me see …" He pretended to examine the papers on her desk, at the same time pulling her swivel chair away from it.

"A beautiful, efficient woman deserves to have some leisure time. You work too hard. I'm not going to be blamed for being a tyrant." He touched her shoulder, kissed her hair.

She recoiled, flinching away from his kiss, dropping the shoulder he had just touched.

He came slowly around in front of the desk. He smiled his dazzling, carefree smile.

All Cleo could think about was the warm scent of him, a scent she loved now but had never known before. She wanted to take his hands from the desk where he was leaning and smother them with kisses. She tried to gain control of her ragged breathing.

She said, her voice almost a whisper, "Thank you for the roses; they're beautiful. But it is not my birthday." She looked down, hoping to maintain some decorum.

"I know it's not your birthday, but to me it's the birth of something wonderful, so I'm calling it your birthday." His voice was like soft waves over smooth rock.

"Dr. Blanchard—Jimmy, I don't know what to say. I'm very busy today." But her defenses were irrelevant. "Jimmy," she pleaded, "I'm looking for some quiet time. I need some time to think."

"I'll close the door again, if you wish, and give you all the space you need, but only if you promise to keep our dinner date tonight."

Cleo just looked at him and shook her head, for in spite of her attraction to him, her gut feeling was telling her no.

Jimmy pushed the papers away and sat on the corner of the desk. Lifting her chin so that he looked into her eyes, he said in a whisper, "I know it's about Saturday. I apologize for my behavior. You just don't have any idea of your power, girl. I lost my senses, and I'm asking you to forgive me."

"Jimmy, I don't know what to do. You just make me—I don't think …"

"Sweetheart, don't think, trust me. I care about you, Cleo, and I would never hurt you."

Cleo looked up at him boldly and said, "But I might hurt you. Did you ever think of that?"

He was surprised by her words, but he folded both her hands in his and, kissing them, said gently, "Just dinner, that's all I ask. I promise, it won't happen again, I swear to God! Forgive me, please?"

Cleo looked for a long time into his eyes and then said, haltingly, "All right, then. I forgive you."

Without releasing her hands, Jimmy bent low, his face close to hers, and said, his voice full of sincerity and passion, "I care about you, Cleo, and I will always respect your wishes. I promise." His eyes explored her face more intimately than was polite or necessary. "I'll see you tonight then?"

"Yes."

"I'll pick you up here at 5:30."

Cleo gave him no smile and dismissed him with her eyes.

After Jimmy closed the door, Cleo sighed in resignation but was buoyed by a brave inner voice saying, *I can handle him. I'll see him only where there are others around and here at work. I just won't allow him in my house again. After all, I like my job, and he's quite well thought of here, so there's no reason not to go out socially with him—occasionally.*

CHAPTER THIRTEEN

D R. JIMMY BLANCHARD ALSO seemed out of place in Springhill, but he was accepted and admired. He was considered the "golden boy," a great man-about-town, and a genius at the hospital. And his charm was legendary. He spoke in an accent that was a perfect marriage of British and Barbadian. Lean, tall, and muscular, his masculine energy radiated so mysteriously about him that women were drawn to him, wanted to move into his sizzling aura, give their love to him on the spot. He wasn't the most handsome man in town—he just had that way about him.

Men liked him, too. He knew how to jive with them or tell a great story. He knew how to use what he had to get what he wanted. And he knew now that Cleo was the first woman he had wanted this badly in a very long time.

There were few social activities available for single men in Springhill, other than those interminable feasts at the homes of black families, hosted by the elite members of the town's Negro society. And for all his dignified pretensions, Jimmy Blanchard had cast smoldering eyes on a number of the women around town, but the easiest and least complicated place to satisfy his voracious sexual appetite was in Brickhouse Row, an alley of commercial buildings behind the railroad tracks, close to Smitty's Barbecue Shack and next to Brinson's Liquors, where a man could find anything he wanted—girls, whisky, food, and jukebox jazz that kept couples jumping all night long. A handsome, single doctor in a small town like Springhill naturally aroused curiosity. Brickhouse Row was derided by the better class of Negroes. But Jimmy liked the atmosphere—it reminded him of Barbados. He couldn't risk taking a woman to his apartment in the duplex he shared with a local barber. Cleo required special treatment.

At the appointed hour of their dinner date, Jimmy knocked on Cleo's office door. He was the epitome of politeness and respect as he escorted Cleo to his car, with the hospital staff returning their smiles. Almost bowing to Cleo, he opened the passenger side and assisted her into the seat of his luxurious Packard sedan, polished to the hilt. He drove out on the highway and out of town.

Cleo asked, hoping there was no hint of fear or concern in her voice, "So, what are we doing—taking a drive before dinner?"

Jimmy looked sideways at her and said, "I just felt you deserved more than a shack for dinner. The place I'm taking you is quite comfortable and beautiful, with music we can dance to—that is, if you wish."

This brought a smile to Cleo's face, but she said, "I'm not dressed for a party."

"Don't worry, you look absolutely beautiful. I love the way you're dressed."

After driving some distance, they came to a beautiful, white stucco building situated next to a river. The façade was covered with vines, which were festooned with what looked like thousands of small Christmas lights. They had to cross the bridge over the inlet to get to it.

"What is this place?" Cleo asked, looking at the abundant palm trees placed in huge pots throughout the rooms. Large glass windows brought the outside foliage in, causing Cleo to gasp aloud at the effect. It was like a tropical oasis.

They passed through a room where tables were set with white damask tablecloths on which formal silver settings were laid. In the next room—a more informal setting—a Negro band was playing jazz, and beautifully dressed couples were dancing, holding each other closely, their hips as well as their feet keeping time to the music.

Cleo asked to be excused as they passed a powder room. In the privacy of the room, she removed her jacket, quickly unpinned and let down her hair, and put makeup on her face. She unbuttoned her white blouse so that her throat was exposed, and the collar was now draped slightly off her shoulders. She was glad she had chosen a flared skirt. The exciting events had brought a rosy glow to her face, and her long, wavy hair enhanced its delicate contours.

Jimmy was waiting just outside for her near a potted palm, and when she came toward him, he gave her an admiring look, and Cleo knew he was pleased with the small changes she had made in her appearance. A man wearing a tuxedo escorted them to a table near the front where couples were seated surrounding the orchestra.

"Do you know anyone in this crowd?" Cleo asked, as they rose to dance the last dance before dinner. She was so proud to be here with such a fine-looking man that she kept smiling up at him, thinking how much she loved to look into his eyes, which seemed always on her, solicitous and admiring.

"No, in fact, they've just taken me on as a member. This is only my first visit here. But let's dance, and then I'll give you a history lesson, if you want, of how this place came to be."

Several couples cast admiring glances as they made their way to the raised dance floor near the bandstand. People all around them appeared friendly and courteous.

They danced closely, for this was a slow number, and Cleo felt his muscles even through his jacket. Pulling back with both hands on his arms, she asked, "How did you get such strong arm muscles?"

"Every single summer I came back from school to Barbados and worked on my grandfather's farm. My usual job was to unload sugarcane from the wagons and help the farmhands tie stalks into tight bundles. My father never allowed me to use the machetes to cut the cane, but I did my share of harvesting. In fact, I worked there every summer until I finished medical school. I wasn't always happy about having to work so hard, but, like they say, 'All's well that ends well.'" He held her more tightly in his arms. "See?"

Cleo felt secure in his arms, soothed by the band's music. She could feel his warmth, even hear his heart beating, and she smelled that wonderful scent that was so masculine and distinctly his.

When the band took a break, Jimmy went over and shook hands with the band members, complimenting them and discussing their distinctive style of music. Cleo stood back waiting for him to return. Then, searching his eyes for clues, she said, "Tell me about this place."

Jimmy leaned toward her and explained, "This is a wealthy, private club for Negro gentlemen and their ladies. Most of the members are professional men—doctors, lawyers, teachers, and businessmen. It's called the Forum, and it was actually begun by West Indians who came here in 1919. Very proper people, m'lady. Would you like to go out to the terrace?"

Cleo took his arm as they crossed the little bridge over a moat to the club's outdoor terrace and stood there watching the water lapping against the river's bank. Cleo snuggled closer to him, feeling she was in a fairyland.

After returning to their table, they sat silently listing to the wonderful music. They were both tapping their fingers on the table to the beat of "The King Porter Stomp," the surging rhythm adding to their obvious pleasure in being together in such a place.

After dinner, the musicians took it up a notch. The Blue Barons now launched into a fast rendition of "Jumpin' at the Woodside," the piano cutting away in a kind of panic, with the tenor sax pursuing its beat with vigilance.

Taking Cleo by the hand, Jimmy said, "Let's turn this place out!"

Cleo and Jimmy walked onto the dance floor and launched into a fast dance, creating new steps—some from the West Indies, others from ballet, every one as classic as the orchestra's jazz improvisations. They danced with complete abandon. Jimmy lifted Cleo off her feet and into the air, her flared skirt floating above her beautiful legs, as she swirled back and forth, until at last Jimmy took her down and backward on the final note. It was only then that Cleo noticed a crowd had formed to watch them, and they were now applauding loudly.

Cleo was so delighted she had found a soul mate, someone who loved music and dance as much as she did. On the final slow number, the Blue Barons' theme song, "Dear Old Southland," Cleo melted into Jimmy's arms as they moved slowly to the clarinet's lovely phrasing. Jimmy whispered in Cleo's ear, "One day I'll take you to New Orleans for the real thing."

Many couples came up and introduced themselves, some asking Cleo if she was a professional dancer. She replied that she had studied with a great teacher since the age of ten.

Jimmy led Cleo to the bandstand, asking the band about their tour and talking about jazz.

After that evening, dinner and dancing at the Forum on the river became their weekend ritual. As time passed, Cleo looked upon their courtship and at Jimmy in a different way. He was her knight in shining armor, and she was his ladylove.

CHAPTER FOURTEEN

JIMMY WANTED TO BE Cleo's protector, and at the same time he wanted to be her lover. The difficulty was that he was indebted to the Wallaces for his position at the hospital, and Cleo was considered a member of their family. She was the Wallaces' protégée, and if he hurt her it could well be the end of his entire career.

Cleo seemed to respect him now, but getting her attention in a sexual way would require careful handling on his part. Jimmy decided to make no sexual advances that she did not initiate. His passion for Cleo had never subsided since that Saturday he made his first advances, and he realized that, although she appeared cool and reserved on the outside, her arduous response to him proved that a burning caldron of sexual desire lay within.

Jimmy knew he could no longer risk patronizing the town's low-down haunts with their ever-changing parade of fleshy pleasures. And as Cleo grew on him, his curiosity was continually aroused. He was determined to figure out what was beneath her outer reserve that could come so quickly alive at the touch of his hands and move so alluringly to the sound of music.

Jimmy knew he had to take some decisive action, because what was once a pleasant pastime and a relief from the boredom of his everyday life had become a bothersome obsession. Cleo had finally entered his dreams and would not leave him alone.

During the Easter holidays, Jimmy Blanchard arranged a trip out of town for them. He wanted a place where they could get away and not be under the watchful eyes of the arbiters of Springhill society. *I need her,* Jimmy thought to himself. *I can't marry her, but I need her to become my own.*

Jimmy had the good luck to learn of a Negro physicians' convention in Savannah, scheduled during the spring holidays. He explained to his staff that he was taking Cleo along to take notes and to reinforce her knowledge of hospital administration.

They began their journey to Savannah the second week in March, with Cordelia's blessings, for they were going to be the guests of Dr. and Mrs. Branch Lafayette, the distinguished Savannah physician and his wife. Jimmy had his Packard cleaned and his seats refurbished for the occasion.

The month of March was colder than usual, so Cordelia gave the couple a warm red, white, and blue quilt her mother had created years ago. Cordelia also packed a huge picnic basket with food. Cleo was looking forward to seeing Louis Armstrong and his band, who were touring the South, including Savannah.

They had reached the halfway mark on their journey to Savannah when Jimmy said, "The smell of that fried chicken is driving me crazy. Let's eat, girl!"

They stopped at a little white church high on a hill, whose steeple they had seen from the highway. The church overlooked a pond bordered by tall swamp weeds with little purple cones on their tops. They spread a blanket; ate ravishingly from the basket of fried chicken, potato salad, cornbread, and apple pie that Cordelia had made; and shared only the pleasant stories of their childhoods.

Afterward, Jimmy rested his head in her lap and she stroked his hair, loving the feel of its short, wiry tangles, kissing his forehead lovingly from time to time as he napped. Later as they drove farther south, the trees became greener, and their buds, tinged with color, signaled that within a few weeks, they would burst into colorful blooms.

But farther on during their journey, the scenes along the road became ugly and foreboding. They passed shacks set up close together with makeshift porches slanting perilously and rusty roofs that were certain to let in both the rain and the heat. Large families with many children walked aimlessly in small bleak yards, and Cleo shuddered when she imagined them going inside for the night and pushing the fragile walls of the decrepit shacks to their limits if all of them tried to seek shelter at once.

Numerous migrant farm workers carrying worn tools walked along the dusty roads, heads bowed, wiping the sweat off their faces with their already dirty and sweaty clothes. Cleo felt guilty that the dust the Packard created added to the misery of these people. Cleo watched a little girl who was alone among a group of women—for most of the other children had run ahead—tagging slowly alongside the wire fence, rubbing her eyes with her shirt and crying loudly. The two boys farther ahead were probably the child's brothers. They looked angry and held handfuls of pebbles and gravel, throwing pieces randomly over the fence and into the field.

Cleo called loudly, "Stop, Jimmy! That little girl in the pink shirt is crying; I think she's hungry. Do you see her? Stop! Let's see if these people need some food. We have lots of food left in our basket."

Jimmy looked warily out the window, slowed down, and then suddenly sped off as they came abreast of the first group of people, saying, "They look … dirty and ignorant. If we stop they might try to get in the car; it's not a good idea." He had left them in a cloud of dust.

"Jimmy, if you don't stop this car, *right now*, and give those people our basket, I'm never going to speak to you again!"

When he noticed Cleo was crying, he asked, "Baby, what's the matter? There's no point in trying to help these few. There are thousands of people out of work now. Our little basket won't help; it won't change their lives one iota. Besides, we don't want to get close. I can smell them even this distance away." He could see Cleo was unimpressed.

Jimmy slowed the car and stopped, then slowly backed up. When the group came abreast of the car, he jumped out of the car and said, "Howdy! My lady and I have a basket of food. We'd like you to take it. There's bread, apples, pie, chicken, and potato salad."

The people seemed filled with shame, bowing and looking down at their feet, but the little girl, still crying, came running down the side of the road toward the car. Cleo jumped out and smiled at her. She held out her hand and said, "What's your name, honey?" The little girl didn't answer but kept looking at the basket Jimmy was holding, tears still running down her cheeks.

Cleo reached into the basket and handed the little girl a biscuit and a piece of chicken. She was so hungry she almost choked on the first piece. By the time Cleo brought out the thermos of lemonade, the whole crowd, including the two older boys, had gathered around.

Jimmy handed them the entire basket, including the thermos of lemonade, and Cleo gave one of the women the hand-made quilt. "Take this for the children. It may get colder later."

By this time, the adults were standing around, smiling mostly toothless smiles, and reaching into the basket. None of the men had taken a bite yet but busied themselves passing the food out to the women and children. They kept saying over and over, "Thank y'all! Thank y'all! God bless y'all!"

Jimmy looked embarrassed as he said, "Uh, well, good-bye, and enjoy the food." Then he reached into his pocket and gave a handful of coins and a couple of bills to the adults who seemed to be the parents of the children. "Maybe y'all can divide that among you."

They waved back at the smiling group, as they got into their car and drove slowly away. Cleo blew kisses to the children, who were too busy eating to respond.

Jimmy drove on through small farming villages, noticing the desolated dry earth and dead foliage, realizing for the first time that there was a serious drought. Cleo slept with Jimmy's trench coat over her, as the weather had turned cooler. Mainly, though, he was preoccupied with planning how he was going to make Cleo completely his own and never let her go. He was concerned that Cleo was her own person and a stronger woman than he had imagined. Cleo handled her work at the hospital in a cool, professional way, completing her jobs efficiently and with attention to every detail, focusing not enough attention on him. He realized that he didn't know where she stood all this time they had been dating. It was a new concern for him. His sense of his own irresistible magnetism was blowing like dust across the fields to an unseen horizon.

CHAPTER FIFTEEN

NO ONE WAS AT the Lafayettes' house when they arrived, so Jimmy unlocked the door and ushered Cleo inside. She was surprised he had a key. Cleo looked around eagerly and was impressed with the Lafayettes' beautifully decorated home. Her high heels sank into the plush carpet as she walked around the sunken living room, inspecting the paintings on the paneled walls. The room, with its cozy, dark brown, wrap-around couches; low oriental tables; and fine drapes and curtains, was the picture of taste and comfort.

Cleo had taken her shoes off, and holding them in her hands, inspected a glass case of African statuary, and a wall of modern art displayed to utmost eloquence in its own special indirect lighting. They toured as if in a museum, discussing the individual merits of the various pieces of art. The living room opened through mahogany double doors into a sumptuous dining room that could easily seat twenty people at its long, highly polished cherry table.

Cleo said, "One day I'd like to have a home like this, wouldn't you?" She held Jimmy's arm and leaned in against him.

Jimmy answered, "If you were in my home, you would be all the ornament I would need."

In the kitchen on the counter was an envelope addressed to "Dr. Blanchard." Upon reading it, Jimmy turned to Cleo and said, "This says that neither Branch nor his wife will be here. They've gone to Atlanta because of his mother's sudden illness. They ask us to make ourselves at home and enjoy all the food and drink they have left for us."

At first, Cleo felt relieved that no one was present, as she was always uneasy and nervous at the ordeal of socializing with strangers, especially when she was tired. She turned toward him and said, "Since you're going to a meeting this afternoon, I think I'll take a nap and then I'll be better able to enjoy the concert tonight."

Jimmy didn't answer but instead took her in his arms and then kissed her lips passionately.

That was when Cleo gently pulled away. She thought, *Of course! He arranged this to get me alone.* She had the dizzying feeling she had been magnificently manipulated. She got up and walked toward the counter.

"May I see the letter?" she asked, her hand reaching for it. After she read it, she added, "That's so generous of them! That's really generous." She threw the letter onto the bar's counter and poured a glass of water, leaning heavily into the sink because she suddenly felt faint.

Jimmy was beside her, his arms around her shoulders. "Are you okay, honey? Why don't you lie down and rest? I don't think I'll go to the meeting this afternoon if you're not feeling well. I'll stay here and work on that speech I'm making tomorrow."

Cleo walked from the room, with Jimmy following closely.

"Jimmy, I do feel like washing up a bit," she said, and turning, she walked quickly into the pink and white bathroom just in front of her and slammed the door. "I'll be right out!" she called through the locked door.

Cleo looked at her flushed face in the mirror, wondering what was wrong with her. "Why am I so suspicious? In the many months since that first Saturday at my house, he's always been a perfect gentleman." She shook her head and splashed her face with water.

"Cleo!" Jimmy called loudly from down the hallway. "There's a large bath in the master bedroom; why not use that one?"

Cleo unlocked the door, looking at Jimmy as he walked down

the hall, water dripping from her face. "You seem to know where everything is in this house! How is that?"

Just as Jimmy sprang toward the bathroom to take her in his arms, Cleo slammed the door and locked it again. Jimmy leaned against the door and said softly, "Cleo, I was best man at their wedding; they're both from Barbados. I've known Branch and Brenda since childhood. I've stayed here many times, like just before I got the job at the hospital, and was waiting for their acceptance."

Cleo felt like a child and managed to whisper through the door, "I'm sorry, Jimmy. I guess I really am too tired to be reasonable. I'll go into the bedroom and lie down for a while."

"I'll take your things in for you." He returned with her suitcase, and Cleo followed him down the hall to another wing of the house.

They entered an immense bedroom with mirrored walls on one side, a room that was obviously the master suite with an adjoining closet/dressing room, and a large double bathroom. Jimmy took her hands, gently drawing her to him. "Cleo, don't you understand that I love you? I'll always take care of you, in every way, and I'll do whatever you want. All you have to do is tell me what to do."

Jimmy crossed to the large bed and turned back the covers for her. She was about to protest when he said, "Take a good rest, honey, as long as you like. I'll go to the dining room and get on with my writing."

Cleo was completely exhausted now, not from the trip but from trying to control her own emotions. The memories of his lips on her breasts flooded over her. She wanted nothing more than to have him hold her close like that again. But over the last few months she had told him of her desire to stay a virgin until marriage. He had agreed with her, telling her that he would wait for her, that he wanted that also.

Now she doubted her own control here alone in the house with him. What would a sophisticated woman do under these circumstances? Every inch of her wanted him, yet she knew instinctively that it would change their relationship into something she was not sure she was prepared to handle. She took off her dress and hung it carefully in the closet. Then she lay down on the bed and thought, *I'll never be able to stay here with him and keep my sanity. Tomorrow I'll take the train back. But I'm too tired to think about it now.*

She fell into a deep sleep. It was very dark outside her window when Jimmy came in to ask if she wanted to go out to eat or see what had been left for them in the refrigerator. She had been dreaming about him. In the dream he was making love to her, and it was like going to heaven.

She instinctively raised her arms to him, and he fell down beside her. She kissed him passionately, and they lay holding each other for a long time. She was surprised when he disengaged himself from her arms and fell to his knees on the floor beside the bed.

From his kneeling position, she could barely see him in the darkness. She turned toward him, lying on her side, as Jimmy reached for her hands and, in a husky voice, said, "Cleo, I love you so much. Cleo, will you marry me? Marry me, please? Today, tomorrow, soon?"

Between his kisses and hers, she said, her voice a murmur filled with passion, "Yes, yes, yes! Oh, my love, yes!"

Cleo lifted herself on her elbows and said, "Before you came in just now, I was dreaming we were making love. It was like floating on the clouds, like no experience I had ever had. Should I be dreaming such a dream?"

Jimmy rose and lay on the bed next to her. He turned to face her, but he made no move, lying very still. He said at last, "I promised you that I would never take advantage of you again. Remember? I've always wanted to make it up to you for that Saturday."

She knew that she was too much in love with him not to touch him. She had to hug him, kiss him, feel his hands on her body and his strong arms around her. She had to accept that—what did they call it in those romance novels? Yes, she accepted it now; she was "hopelessly in love."

She wanted him as she had on that Saturday morning. She wanted to end this terrible throbbing in her groin; she wanted him desperately, needed him, whatever the cost. Her continuing obstinate resistance was not worth the physical longing she felt.

Cleo pulled herself forward, and with one arm across his chest she said, "I love you, Jimmy. I love you so much. I trust you completely." She climbed on top of him, moved her aching body on his in a slow rhythm, and felt him go hard beneath her. "I want you to have me; please take me, Jimmy, please!"

Suddenly, they were each groping the other, taking off each other's garments, and finally sinking back into the bed. Jimmy kissed her entire body—her toes, her vulva, her breasts, her lips—until she was thrashing and moaning, "Please, Jimmy! Please, Jimmy!"

And then their bodies were entangled. Jimmy heard her sighs as if in the distance, as he was steeling himself to hang on, to wait for her; so his thoughts went to that never-forgotten time, his last soccer championship game when his strong body and steely legs had won his team the victory. And then he thought about how he climbed England's steep hills, running on strong legs to the top, never giving up, never letting go—higher and higher—until out of the mist he felt her contractions and her moans, and he plunged with her into the pool far below the mountain slope, and was in her, with her, at that moment when she, too, fell into the abyss.

As for Cleo, she was floating on water lilies in safe waters that cloaked her in wave after wave of warmth; that flowed through her and enveloped her until her body was a sacrament to its own pleasure; that sent her shooting for the stars and blinded her at the moment they exploded inside.

Jimmy kissed Cleo passionately and gently massaged her back until she fell asleep. Later in the night, they were entangled again like vines with flowers that opened and closed until they were exhausted, and by the early morning hours they were finally satisfied.

CHAPTER SIXTEEN

FOR THE FIRST TIME, Cleo felt completely at ease with him, seeing him now without the intensity of her passion clouding her vision. For the first time in their relationship, she talked to him about her lost childhood and her years at the castle. She couldn't yet confess how often she felt unloved and abandoned, or how she longed to have children in order to validate her own existence in the world.

Jimmy, too, was warmer, the tensions connected with the pursuit of her body laid to rest. He, too, shared his childhood. In England he felt the need to excel in competition with his classmates, all white men of the upper social strata. His summers were quite different from theirs; he had to go home and help his family work on the farm while his classmates took vacations abroad.

He told Cleo about his favorite sister, Hattie, four years younger than he, who had given up her chance to pursue a college education so that he could go to medical school. He was the hope of his whole family—the chosen one, who was now expected to do something for them.

One evening as they sat at a center table at the Forum, Jimmy held her hands on the pretense of admiring their softness and slipped an expensive, vintage pearl engagement ring onto her finger. He fell to his knees and asked Cleo to marry him as the band played "Love Will Find a Way." Cleo beamed with pride and pleasure as others looked toward the most romantic couple among them.

For the first time in her life, Cleo began to feel that life was fair after all, that she, an orphan, an unfortunate urchin held in disdain by her parents, would soon become a physician's wife, respected by everyone in the community. She would entertain, have teas, throw dinner parties, and invite others of similar means. And of course, they would not always have to remain in Springhill. He might one day get a position in Atlanta or Chicago.

On one of their Sunday drives, they found a small, beautiful brick house for sale on the edge of the woods where River Street ended at an overgrown path leading into the forest. They ate lunch on the banks of a rushing stream. The following day, Jimmy purchased the property and immediately began clearing the land and making renovations. It would be a place where he and Cleo could spend time alone and re-create the magic of their Savannah sojourn. It was the perfect love nest, with its sheltering trees hidden from public view. They could live in privacy here, far off the beaten path.

In spite of the fact that her engagement ring was ostentatious and she was certain that the Wallaces had seen it, Cordelia and Albert had said nothing. After several weeks, Cleo finally decided to have a frank discussion with them and ask both for their blessings on her upcoming marriage.

One Saturday morning, without announcement, Cleo walked over to the Wallace home and knocked on the large oak door; she went in without waiting for an answer, as was her custom.

Cordelia took Cleo into her arms and said, "I was just going to call to invite you for dinner on Saturday. You must come! All the hospital staff members are coming and you're the guest of honor, of course."

Cleo was encouraged by Cordelia's invitation for dinner. Perhaps she had been too quick to judge them; perhaps this meant that they were going to give her marriage their stamp of approval. "You don't know how much I have missed you. I'll be delighted to come."

"I've missed you, too. Of course, I know you are busy with all the work at the hospital," Cordelia said, as she poured them both coffee and passed her homemade cinnamon buns.

"Well, my work gets easier all the time. I could actually run the place now. It's been two years."

"Hmm, time does fly, doesn't it?"

Finally, Cleo broke the silence. "Cordelia, I wonder if you will help me plan my wedding to Jimmy. I hope we can be married in late summer or early fall at the latest."

Cordelia was about to sip her coffee but now set the cup clumsily in the saucer, almost spilling its contents.

"Cleo, I want to tell you that we love Dr. Blanchard. He's an excellent physician, hand-picked by my husband." Cordelia paused, emitting a long breath, and looked apologetically at Cleo. "But Albert and I feel it's a bit premature to plan your wedding to Jimmy."

Cleo was shocked and felt her face grow hot. This was certainly not what she expected.

"Premature? What are you saying? I know he's a wonderful doctor. I love him very much. I would appreciate your help in planning our wedding." Cleo's face was burning, her eyes watering.

Cordelia drew a deep breath and said, "Cleo, something has come up."

Cleo's instincts told her something was terribly wrong. "What do you have against him? What are you keeping from me?" The questions flew from her mouth like arrows finding their mark.

Cordelia looked at Cleo with eyes close to tears and said, "Cleo, we all must be patient. We will be ready to discuss this later after Albert gets some additional information. Albert was so eager to offer Dr. Blanchard the job that he forgot to get some important background information about him, which could determine whether you should marry him. As soon as that is done, we will talk, I promise."

Cleo looked at Cordelia as if she were a stranger from another planet, exclaiming, "What information? From where?"

Cordelia stood immediately and asked, "Cleo, dear, why do you want to marry at such a young age? Wouldn't you like to wait a little longer before you tie yourself down? You have that trust fund, enough to go to any college that accepts you. Why not think about going away to school?"

The question fell like a balloon losing air. Then Cordelia came over, put her arms around Cleo's shoulders, and said softly and gently, "Cleo, there is a possibility that Jimmy has a wife in Barbados—we are not sure."

Cleo jumped to her feet, exclaiming, "I don't believe this! For some reason none of you want me to be happy!" Then she turned and dashed from the room, running out the front door and slamming it with such force Cordelia thought the glass panel had broken. Cordelia turned and ran to Albert's office to tell him about the awful turn of events. *The burden of being a friend and confidant,* she said to herself. *This is all too much!*

Upon leaving the Wallace home, Cleo went directly to the hospital, where she found Jimmy working on Saturday as usual. She burst into the office, slamming the door noisily in her wake, and confronted him. "How could you deceive me? How could you do this to me?"

Jimmy, taken off guard, rose immediately from his desk, pushed papers vigorously about, and said, "Cleo, what is the matter with you? What are you saying?"

"You never intended to marry me! All you wanted was to get me in bed. Why would you lie to me, tell me you love me? That you want to marry me?"

Jimmy came around his desk and embraced her, taking her into his arms. He kissed her cheeks, which were red and blazing. He held tightly onto her as she squirmed, fought, and tried to push him away. Jimmy held onto her flaying arms, kissed her tears, and cradled her head against his chest. "I have known for some time that the Wallaces were digging up my long-past history in Barbados. I think what misled them is something that happened a long time ago and is now over and done with. When I was seventeen, I married this woman and she had a child. The child is not mine, but she threatened me and I was vulnerable. What did I know at that age? This woman claimed I conceived her child out in a sugarcane field, of all places. Her father threatened me with bodily harm if I didn't marry her. I wanted a career, and when I went back to England, my father annulled the marriage and I entered medical school. I have never seen or heard from her or her family since. I promise you, I am not now married. I will prove it to you. You are my life, my love, my only love, and my future wife. Don't let others come between us. We have to hang onto each other, against all opposition."

Jimmy wiped her tears away and told her he loved her, that lies would not change their feelings as long as they remained strong and steady. Tomorrow, he promised, he would file the proper legal marriage documents. They would set the date. Let others be damned!

That day, Cleo decided she would move into his house; she didn't care who talked about her, who called her a "tramp," or any other despicable word they would use to put them down.

However, by the following morning Cleo was less sure of what course to take in order to maintain the support of the Wallaces, who had always helped her in the past. She decided to be patient, as Cordelia had suggested, and soon she would discover whether Jimmy was legally married. That was her only path to the big church wedding with the pomp and ceremony that she envisioned.

Albert reviewed all the documentation on Dr. Blanchard's records they had on hand. He had listed himself as "single" on his applications, and his sister, Hattie Burton, a prominent beautician on Chicago's South Side, was his sponsor. Alice King's coworker at Chicago University happened to be one of Hattie's beauty parlor clients. The Wallaces wrote a letter of introduction to Hattie, stating their good fortune in having recruited her brother for the position of surgeon and administrator of the Springhill Memorial Hospital.

Thus began a flurry of letters and telephone calls, back and forth, between Hattie Burton and the Wallaces, leading inevitably to the full disclosure of Jimmy Blanchard's circumstances. He was indeed married with a wife, Deidre, and two boys, who attended school in England.

Cordelia and Albert were devastated by these findings. They loved

Jimmy, and Cleo was like one of their own children. They decided that Albert would confront Jimmy with the revelations, man to man.

The next morning, Albert made an appointment to meet with Jimmy at the hospital. When Albert revealed his reason for the visit, Jimmy turned ashen, then sat on his desk, his head in his hands. When he finally looked up, he seemed more shaken and vulnerable than Albert had ever seen him.

"I know it may be hard for you to believe, but I truly love Cleo and I know she loves me. Please allow me the dignity of telling her myself."

Albert reluctantly agreed to give him time, and without saying another word, turned away, closing the door behind him.

Albert and Cordelia waited, but days and then weeks went by with no indication that Jimmy had told Cleo of his situation. There was no more talk of a wedding and Cordelia sensed that Cleo was afraid to broach the subject. After many long discussions, Albert and Cordelia decided not to inject themselves further into the young couple's destiny.

CHAPTER SEVENTEEN

A T THE END OF May 1936, Oscar, Audrey, and Ophelia sat on a train headed to Springhill for summer vacation. The South was experiencing a blistering heat wave and drought. The overpowering heat turned people into the streets, seeking breezes under shady trees, but only a rare gust held its course in this hot, withering air. The racial climate had also worsened. The three young people, home from the intellectual stimulation of their schools in Atlanta, had grown wiser over the years, enlightenment bringing with it the inevitable acknowledgment of truth. Oscar, especially, felt there was little hope for Negroes to achieve any kind of equity in the South in the near future.

Oscar looked at the girls sleeping fitfully, Audrey cuddled against his shoulder and Ophelia lying across two seats. Looking at them brought back memories of the happy life he enjoyed growing up with his family. But when he glanced out at the hills, a blur of dusky streaks, he thought again of how shocked he was when he became man enough to accept the actual facts of black people's dismal existence in this country. His parents had seemed to expect that talent and education would save all of them from that existence.

Oscar's goal to become a civil rights lawyer brought him in contact with others with the same ambitions. At school like-minded students and faculty banded together, attended meetings and political lectures, and argued the merits of current civil rights cases. Oscar's professors spoke of the hope they once had in FDR's leadership, especially for an anti-lynching bill that he supported, and which had seemed imminent. But a congressional filibuster caused the bill to die in the Senate. Oscar had attended a lecture by First Lady Eleanor Roosevelt and Mary McLeod Bethune, a Negro educator. Together they called for the end of the lawless vigilante groups that were roaming the countryside looking for Negro blood. Instead of listening to their message, the rednecks castigated Mrs. Roosevelt for having her picture taken with Negroes and for riding in a car with Mrs. Bethune.

Most of the civil rights lawsuits showed that Negroes, accused in most instances of crimes they did not commit, could not get a fair trial in any southern court. Already in the year just past, there had been more than twenty lynchings of black men and women. Oscar attended lectures in which he and his fellow students debated ways to guarantee civil rights, but they learned that in order to achieve minimum goals, they would have to fight the police, the mayors, the governors, and all the other southern leaders, most of whom belonged to the Klan.

Oscar could barely breathe, he felt so angry and disgusted. The putrid air, filled with the bad will that was the soul of the white South, was stifling. He looked at the two beautiful, innocent girls, his sister and Audrey, and felt sad and disillusioned. He sat looking through the dirty windows at the hard, red, unyielding earth, and remembered the magnolia blossoms he loved so much along his parents' garden fence, which would never seem the same to him, would be closed forever to him, their soft blossoms repelled from showing their beauty to him in this interminable hellhole.

Into this dense and oppressive racial climate, Oscar invited Abe Swartz to visit them. Abe Swartz was his mentor and one of the lawyers working on the Scottsboro Boys' defense team. In fact, it was Abe's impressive work that had inspired Oscar to become a civil rights lawyer. Swartz was also helping Oscar investigate law schools that he might attend. He was driving down to Georgia from New York later.

Abe Swartz was so impressed with Oscar's abilities that he told him he was a shoo-in for the law school at Columbia University in New York. Abe Swartz had been one of the main organizers of the farmers' unions in the South. He was talented, erudite, and scholarly. He was also a Communist from New York City.

When Oscar informed his mother that he was bringing not only Audrey, but also Abe as houseguests, she was rather at a loss to maintain her usual courteous composure. Even though she knew Abe was white, her first reaction was to say, "Of course, invite your professor to be our houseguest."

But before she could get the words out of her mouth, Oscar said, "He's staying at a hotel in town, but Mom, can we invite him to dinner?"

Cordelia was relieved and said, "Of course, invite your professor for dinner." She had heard of Abe Swartz from Albert and supported his work for civil rights. But she was ill at ease, knowing the volatile climate that existed between the races in Springhill.

Oscar also invited Emmett Lansing from New York City, who had spent many vacations with him. Emmett would be in Springhill for only a short visit, for he had a summer job as a student intern with a New York newspaper.

When Abe arrived in a flashy green Oldsmobile, Albert was barbecuing a whole pig on a spit on the grounds of the abandoned Normal School, which the neighbors were using as a park since no one had yet laid claim to it. Cordelia was in the steamy kitchen preparing potato salad, succotash, string beans, biscuits, and grated sweet potato pudding. Picnic tables were set up out on the school's playgrounds. At the moment, probably because of the heat, everyone was clamoring around a large washtub filled with ice, cold drinks, and watermelons, relishing the cool air rising from the tub.

Abe brought with him a young white woman, Ruby Bates, and they struck up a conversation with Ed Featherstone, the farmer whose pig, already dressed and stuffed, Abe was eyeing with some trepidation. Harold Staley reassured Abe that there was a variety of vegetables and salads available if he did not want to eat pork. Abe was making a pitch for the farmers' union, gesturing dramatically and speaking loudly so as to draw others into his circle. Ruby Bates sat quietly most of the time, appearing a bit uneasy in this company.

Cleo was in animated conversation with Mrs. Redd, thanking her again for giving her the little apartment in her home and asking her about Gwen, who was in rehearsals for the Broadway opening of *Carib Song*, Katherine Dunham's new musical.

Matthew was telling Emmett, who was taking copious notes, stories of his travels with the Fisk Jubilee Singers. Ophelia and Audrey were dancing to the music from a radio set up on the grounds, with a long cord running over the hedge into Albert's office. They were snapping their fingers and dancing a jazzy new step called the "jitterbug."

The Wallaces sat near Abe and Ruby Bates, sensing that, although all their guests were friendly, they might ignore them because they were strangers to the town; they were also white. Ruby Bates sat mute, almost as if in a state of shock, in spite of Cordelia's usual gift for dispelling inhibitions. They needn't have worried about Abe, for after they introduced Abe to Harold Staley, neither one could stop talking, so involved were they both with the welfare of the tenant farmers. Later when Christine Crowley walked in with some dessert pies, Ruby became more animated, probably thinking she was white, for she was just about the whitest-looking Negro one would ever see.

Abe was such a forceful speaker for the rights of Negroes that by the end of dinner, with dusk upon them, most people were gathered around him at his table, some standing and some sitting, to hear what he had to say. Abe was a fascinating man with a keen intellect, as knowledgeable about politics in Washington as he was of the plight of the poor and disadvantaged. Later, some people were whispering behind his back that Abe's ulterior motive was to recruit members for the Communist Party, but the Wallaces were keeping an open mind while asking a number of questions. After all, Abe seemed to be on their side.

After dessert, Featherstone brought forth his ukulele and played country music, farming songs, and plantation blues, inspiring many to sing along. The group lingered longer outside in the large open yard than the Wallaces had expected, where everyone seemed to be enjoying the camaraderie and the pleasure of the late evening breezes.

The next day at noon, Abe Swartz and Ruby Bates came by the Wallaces to pick up Oscar, Ophelia, Audrey, and Cleo for their trip to Isaac's house. Emmett and Matthew were coming later. They drove to the castle, but Abe had not realized how far the journey through the woods would be. The heat hung low in the air, pressing down on them, slowing their pace. The dark clouds signaled showers, hopefully later in day. They were quieter than usual, possibly because of the white girl, as they made their way through the pines and an occasional oak grove, whose usual sprightly moss now hung limp and lifeless. Ruby looked downright scared hanging onto Abe's arm, looking around with frightened eyes as if something evil would reach out and disappear with her into the deep thicket of the woods.

Abe loosened his collar and kept complaining that nobody had told him it was so far. He was not dressed for summer, certainly not dressed for this stroll through the woods; his white long-sleeved shirt, stiff with starch, had pieces of leaves and stems sticking to it, and his hat was a little too large for his head. He was tightly hugging his gray suit coat, which he should have left in the car.

Oscar waited for Abe and Ruby to catch up with him, feeling sorry for them, thinking how he would feel if he were outnumbered by a gang of white people walking through the woods. He was leaning over backward to make Ruby and Abe comfortable, telling them he had been coming up here all his life, before it became deserted except for Isaac's house.

Trying to reassure them that the woods were safe, Oscar called back to them as he led the way, "I never saw anything bigger than a frog in the ponds, a rabbit in the thicket, and a hawk on the wing. Oh, I have seen some possums with those wide sweet eyes looking straight at you, hanging upside down by their tails!" But he couldn't resist adding, "But I forgot to mention the water moccasins!"

As they looked anxiously toward the ground for snakes, Oscar yelled, "We're almost there, look over those trees!" There were audible sighs of relief and the usual exclamations of awe and surprise as they saw the dome above the trees. "Every time I see that, even though I've seen this place many times," Oscar said, "I just feel this lump welling up in my throat, and my heart beats faster."

Isaac greeted the group with his usual charming blend of hospitality and effusiveness, speaking with each person as if he or she were the most important person in his universe, asking each about how their lives were going and offering cold Coca-Colas.

Abe asked Isaac the usual questions, and by now Isaac was accustomed to drawing designs in the sand. Oscar assisted Isaac in showing Abe and Ruby around the house and the grounds.

When they returned, Oscar explained the program for the afternoon, which included Isaac's request for more information regarding the Scottsboro Boys' case, and then poetry and music by members of the group, followed by dinner and refreshments. Finally, everyone looked toward Abe, who was sitting where the rosy afternoon light added a tinge of ruddiness to his pale skin.

Abe spoke in a forceful, steady voice, different from his farmer's vernacular last night, as everyone in the room became quiet so they would not miss a word. He began his discourse, not so much about the Scottsboro case itself but about the history of events leading to the case: "The Scottsboro case has been on everyone's lips, and much you have heard are rumors, the truth distorted and bent into various shapes and shades, depending on the political leanings of the persons speaking."

Abe's face tightened, the deep lines in his forehead becoming more noticeable. "And now I want to speak to you about the real facts of the Scottsboro Case. First, I am honored to introduce Ruby Bates. I am Ruby's lawyer. I'm from New York City, the same as Emmett here, and I came down South to help out in the case." Abe gestured toward Ruby, who was looking down at her hands and squirming in her seat.

"You may have read about the young white woman who was brave enough to publicly recant the story of her rape by a group of young black boys, a lie that continues to be promulgated by her friend, who has refused since to say a word in public.

"Ruby is an extraordinary woman, a young woman who made a mistake and wants to rectify it. We had her under twenty-four-hour protection in Atlanta because she was threatened with death many times for telling the truth. It's hard to believe that people still want to put those young boys to death, when they did nothing more than ride in the boxcar of a freight train, looking for work like thousands of poor people, white and black, who must leave their homes to find jobs.

"As you know, the Scottsboro Boys' defense is being paid for by the United States Communist Party, the only organization fighting in our courts for their liberty, as well as the rights of Negroes in the United States.

"The Scottsboro Boys' defense brings up an important factor influencing the outcome of any jury trial of blacks in the South, and that is that a black person accused of a crime cannot get a fair trial. Since Negroes are excluded from jury lists, how in hell can a black person ever get a fair trial? All the juries here in the South consist of only white people, most of whom are avid racists and members of the Ku Klux Klan. What I have gone through in trying to defend these young people—why, it's almost incomprehensible." Abe had spoken passionately but now appeared embarrassed as he looked down with a shy smile and said, "I didn't mean to make such a long speech. Thanks, Isaac, for your warm hospitality, and to all of you." Abe sat and wiped his forehead with a large handkerchief, as if completely spent.

Oscar strode across the room and stood looking down at Abe with a hand on his shoulder, announcing, "One man Abe expertly defended was my friend and classmate, Eddie, who was only passing out leaflets advertising a student meeting, when he was beaten and arrested. So you see why I'm proud of what Abe is doing to help all of us. If my friend had waited for the NAACP to take a stand, he would either be wasting away in jail or hanging from a tree!"

Matthew took the floor and said, "I'm just a musician, but I think there is more all of us can do to change the course of history. I've always believed that if we had taken up John Brown's call and carried it forward, and fought to the death for our own freedom, we would be respected today instead of begging for the crumbs from a lean table seventy or so years after the Emancipation Proclamation."

Emmett jumped to his feet and thrust his fist in the air as if leading an army forward, saying, "We have to take some matters into our own hands, brothers. Our fight is for the same rights fought for in the Revolutionary War—freedom to live like men in a free society."

Oscar added, "When a people do not have the right to vote, do not have the right to jobs, do not have fairness in the court system, and when you have the U.S. Senate upholding the rights of vigilante groups to lynch people, well, I tell you if that doesn't change very soon, they will wipe our race off the face of the earth. Unless we fight back!"

Audrey reached over and patted Oscar's back. There were tears in her eyes.

Abe sat quietly during the moment of silence after Oscar's words and said, "Perhaps you have questions. There are different opinions, of course, always. And they are welcome. I felt it necessary to set the stage for what I am all about, a stranger in town, organizing tenant farmers into unions to fight against those who are, today, trying to enslave scores of farmers."

All appeared to have been deeply affected by the discourse, and expressions of concern clouded their countenances. There were many questions asked that afternoon, as well as skepticism regarding solutions. It seemed that no single answer satisfied the group's hope that Negroes would be accepted as equals in American society. They questioned the efficacy of the Communists to lead them, yet they were the only white organization working toward the goal of civil rights for all people. They sat in silence, heads hung, buried in their thoughts.

Oscar asked Isaac for permission to explain the remainder of the program—one that the young people had prepared from his suggestions the last time they met: that is, that each person would present something personal and creative to the group.

"We have learned a great deal from you, Abe," Oscar said. And walking over to Ruby, he asked, "Would you like to present something, Ruby?" Oscar looked into her eyes in a soothing way, hoping to bring her out of her shell.

Obviously shy and feeling put on the spot, Ruby looked around in a frightened way and then finally said softly, "I'll try to a little later."

Oscar said, "Let us begin," sounding formal as if leading a band. Everyone grew silent, looking expectantly at him, standing tall and handsome, always the correct, dependable leader. Of course, he was constantly trying to impress Audrey, who, as always, couldn't keep her eyes off him.

"First, our distinguished host, the Big Man, the sage, the genius, the eminent architect, and the host of the woods, the one and only, Isaac Naylor!" Oscar now, as animated as a circus impresario, raised his arm toward Isaac, who had seemed until this moment cozy and contented to watch the others from his "throne" by the massive fireplace.

Isaac appeared so reluctant and surprised that everyone laughed as he cautiously came out of the corner beside the fireplace.

"My dear friends, you make my life beautiful and worthwhile. Best of all, you have taught me a new way to live—that one soul can link his soul to others for the good of all, now, and throughout eternity. Thank you for teaching this former hermit a divine lesson on the value of community and camaraderie."

With that, Isaac bowed to the applause of the group and their loud "Bravos." Oscar said, "Thank you, Isaac, for being our friend. Let's make a toast to Isaac, our friend and mentor." Everyone responded by holding Coca-Colas high and drinking large gulps.

Ophelia volunteered to be next, saying timidly, "Please accept my poor attempt at writing this poem." She squared her shoulders and spoke in a strong voice:

He played in the park, a fine young lad with fleeting feet;

Could run so fast, but they caught him at last.

Only twelve years old when they hung him fast

From the old willow tree.

He sang words of praise in his church boy's choir,

His father's black knight; his mother's delight.

When he returned the smile of a blonde-haired girl

The devils in hoods hung him from the old willow tree.

As Ophelia bowed and accepted the thunderous applause, there were tears streaming down her face. Oscar was concerned and slipped her his handkerchief.

He thought, *Ophelia is such a lovely sister, and so gifted and beautiful. She always stands back, not exactly shy, but with regard for others around her. She had practiced her elocution all week, and I criticized her over-dramatization. But it seems to have worked, and she should be very pleased.*

Oscar said loudly for all to hear, "Brilliant, Ophelia," and others followed suit. Oscar was happy, for she usually got little if any praise at all. Oscar thought he must try to be a better big brother and give her more credit. "Our brothers are hanging from trees all over the South," he said. "We need to talk about this. We need to let our voices ring, and not hide our feelings! Thanks, Ophelia."

Suddenly, Ruby Bates was on her feet, tears streaming down her face, wringing her hands, saying, "Please, I'm sorry, I never meant y'all harm; I never meant them boys no harm. I'm a poor girl, down on my luck, and that's why my friend and I hopped that train, and I just …" She buried her head in her arms and sobbed.

Abe Swartz rushed to her side and put his arms around her shoulders. He patted her back, murmuring words of comfort to her as her loud sobs filled the room.

As Abe noticed all the surprised faces looking at Ruby, he said,

"Ruby is one of the bravest women I know. Her story—the story of her life—is a long, sad one, and she'll tell that story when she is stronger. She's traveled all over the South explaining to anyone who would listen that the Scottsboro Boys did not rape her or her friend. Ruby was brave enough to challenge those lies and to tell the truth."

Abe stood alone now, having quieted Ruby's sobs, although she still sat with her reddened face buried in her hands, rocking back and forth. Abe glanced at her and handed her his handkerchief. Ruby wiped her tears and looked at the group in a stricken way. In the next moment, she jumped up, walked with sloping shoulders to the middle of the room, and said in a loud, whiny voice, "Please forgive me, y'all; I'm saved now and I told the truth! Forgive me, Lord, for my sins!"

Abe helped Ruby to her seat as Isaac rushed toward her with a glass of water in his hand. But Ruby was on the floor, her body jerking with convulsions. Cleo rushed to cover Ruby with one of several Indian blankets that lay on the circular bench. Isaac bent on a knee and gave her several gulps of water. Ruby finally said, "I'm okay. Thanks y'all."

Cleo said, "Well, since I'm up, I'll go next, since spirituals soothe the heartfelt soul. I have chosen a song that I hope will depict our dedication to fighting for freedom and happiness for all people."

Everyone nodded in agreement, obviously welcoming a break from the awkward dilemma that had stymied their planned presentations. Cleo stood now, the fading sunlight's glow highlighting her lovely features.

She smiled and said, "Please feel free to join and sing with me whenever the spirit moves you. The song is 'Go Down, Moses,' that great freedom song, and you all know the words."

Holding her hands in the classic style, clutched together out in front of her chest, Cleo began singing, "When Israel was in Egypt land, let my people go. Oppressed so hard they could not stand. Let my people go."

Oscar jumped up, hands in the air, and began directing the others, who joined in the chorus:

"Go down, Moses, way down in Egypt land."

An alien sound rang out. The sound was like an old dry pine tree whose limbs were worn with age, crashing onto the rocks. Even so, no one wanted to stop the singing, having jumped to their feet on "Go down, Moses," singing along with spirit and enthusiasm, moved by the occasion and the deep sentiment of the words.

"Tell ole Pharaoh, let—"

Another sound came closer, shattering something just outside in the yard, perhaps striking tin or metal.

Oscar moved forward toward the others, leaving Cleo suddenly exposed as shots were fired through the window. By the third blast, everyone had realized it was not a falling tree creating the racket. Isaac yelled, "Get down, NOW, flat on the floor!"

Unaware, and still into her presentation, Cleo started to begin the next verse. Emmett rushed across the room, jumping over a chair, and pulled Cleo down just as the bullets ripped through her. Oscar came forward then and narrowly escaped a bullet that whizzed over his head.

The people firing the shots were just outside the window, but there was a lull as Isaac jumped from the floor, ran to the hall, and hit a switch that turned off the lights inside and turned on the outside lights, some on the clearing, others in the trees, others dangling around the adobe's rooftop. Isaac yelled, "The Ku Klux Klan!"

Isaac ran and grabbed one of his rifles from above the fireplace, and before opening the door, he yelled, "Everyone, stay down, don't move an inch; I'm going to get these bastards."

He ran outside and saw that his house was surrounded by masked men in white robes. Isaac fired a few shots into the air, and backing up to the door, he said in a hoarse whisper, "Oscar, crawl out the back way, the way I showed you."

Isaac guarded the door as Abe and Emmett, bending as low as they could, lifted Cleo and supported her upper body while Matthew and Audrey held her feet and legs. Ophelia and Ruby helped support Cleo's spine and middle back, and they carried Cleo swiftly down the steps toward the cellar door. Oscar and Audrey guided the others along through the secret doors and narrow passageways that Isaac had shown them on their earlier visit. After they entered the cellar area, they secured the doors, and then, following Oscar, they proceeded down the secret cellar steps and into a large area where herbs of all kinds filled large containers around a circular room. They were labeled and categorized by their contents and their medicinal usages.

More shots were heard from outside, sounding like distant thunder to those inside the lower space, but no one knew for sure what was happening, only that they had to help Cleo, who was bleeding profusely. Oscar ripped off his white shirt and tore it into strips; he asked Audrey to tie tourniquets around Cleo's injured thigh, while Ruby held a folded linen tablecloth to her damaged pelvic area. Cleo's eyes were open, but she looked as if she was unconscious or in a state of severe shock.

Emmett and Abe were rummaging along the shelves looking for healing herbs; luckily, all the herbs were labeled. Matthew put a pot of water to boil on the wood stove and fired it up. He pulled down wintergreen liniment, and the women followed the directions for rubbing the substance onto Cleo's legs and arms and any area where there were no cuts visible, hoping that this would improve circulation and keep blood flowing to all her organs.

All the women worked desperately on Cleo's arms and legs, rubbing upward and saying soothing words at the same time, and at last Cleo began to speak incoherently; her moans told them she was obviously in great pain. Matthew and Emmett arranged the herbs on cloths, as they followed Oscar's directions, which he read from the labels on the bottles. Finally they tried a remedy labeled "pain reliever," consisting of raspberry leaves and the powdered roots of bistort. They increased their massage efforts, patting and stimulating Cleo's hands, arms, and feet.

They covered her with several blankets they found in a locker, yet she continued to shiver. Matthew found some brandy and forced Cleo to sip a little, which seemed to help immediately. The color returned to her skin, and her body gradually warmed. They all hovered around her so closely that Oscar warned them they were taking her oxygen and needed to give her some space. They moved away a bit but kept talking to her all the time, pleading with her to fight courageously, to stay awake, to breathe.

Outside, the movement of white robes struck a macabre dance in the shadows as the men darted back and forth among the trees on all sides of the adobe house.

Isaac stood outside and yelled to the devils, "I surrender, come and get me. Everyone else has gone, away off yonder!" He gestured emphatically, pointing in the opposite and wrong direction. He walked farther out into the dark woods, continuing to invite the men to take him, hoping to divert their attention from the others, whom he hoped were on their way to safely.

He forced them deep into the woods by walking forward as the men backed up, they were obviously awed by his unbelievable size. Isaac was finally surrounded on all sides by a group of about thirty men. He threw his gun to the ground, held his hands up, and yelled at the top of his voice, "I'm not armed!" Now his hands were high above his head. "Come get me!" He watched as the robes billowed in the wind, coming toward him like legless, floating ghosts.

Flashlights were turned on him and a few of the cloaked men came closer but immediately backed away, probably not believing that this man was real. Finally, following orders from a slight man who appeared to be their leader, several surrounded him, pointing their guns, while others rushed toward him, holding high what looked like a large fishing net, which they billowed upward and, with great effort and after numerous attempts, threw over Isaac, covering him completely from head to toe.

The squeaky-voiced leader pranced about him, yelling, "Looka heah, I believe we got ourselves a nigger gorilla. A real prize gorilla!"

The robed men came cautiously toward Isaac, surrounding him, and tied his hands with rope behind his back. Shortly, most of the others joined in, now feeling more secure, and propelled his body forward with great effort, but the net managed to trip Isaac, and he fell back against an old oak tree. He felt the agony as they struck his body with clubs. Someone threw a rock and hit his face, the flowing blood partially blinding his view of the floating demons.

Isaac began to struggle, using this as a delaying tactic, hoping his young friends had made some headway in getting out of the area. He leaned against the great oak, the sacred tree of his hallowed forest, bleeding all over. Isaac hoped that Oscar remembered the escape route through the underground tunnel that he had showed him. The tunnel had been filled with Indian artifacts when Isaac discovered it and was probably centuries old. Fortunately, it extended all the way to a small path at the farthest barn.

The Klan leader came closer to Isaac and asked him in his high, tremulous voice, "Whar them other niggers, coon?"

Isaac pointed toward the castle and said, "The only road is that way. I think they might have gone to the castle. But please, don't hurt them! They are innocent! Please don't take them, take me instead! I'm the one you want!" Isaac knew the kids would not go to the castle.

One burly man with large feet and swishy, effeminate movements paraded in front of Isaac, hands on his hips, a large diamond ring sparkling in the moonlight. He said, "We seen y'all walking 'round heah wid them white gals lak they yor play thangs. Who the hell ya thank yer are? Throw that in our face, huh? Y'all gonna die fer that right heah, so hep me God! Teach this heah nigger some sense, boys! Show him who in charge!"

Isaac sank to his knees under several blows to the back of his head.

The gang cheered about the great lynching party that would soon ensue with this unusually rare specimen. They boasted at the idea of presenting the Imperial Potentates with this giant trophy, guaranteed to make them celebrities for years to come. They talked about saving him for a real big party, perhaps hiding him until then, in a cell in the castle, along with the others. They talked of calling a special Ku Klux Klan regional picnic, with the Imperial Wizard and the Grand Dragon presiding, thereby ensuring a huge audience and adding all kinds of new converts by putting this huge "nigger" on display.

Soon the others, who had been searching the farm to make sure no one lingered behind, caught up with the rest of the gang and announced, "Wa'll, we gonna get the rest of them niggers later. Couldn't find 'um. Don't know whar they went to. Ain't nowhar to hide 'round heah. Don' worry. Hell, we bound tar git 'um soon."

Another in the group asked, "Who need 'um? We got this giant sonabitch!" The fat man laughed as the thin leader yelled, "Let's go git 'um, boys!" But Isaac was now unconscious, dead weight, lying on the ground. It took the effort of a great many to move him along. They stopped to make a wooden lift with a number of fallen branches tied with ropes, which were in plentiful supply, as was the corn liquor they drank.

The moon hung low in the western sky, as the giant was dragged through the tangled jungle—a divine trophy for the Grand Dragon of the Ku Klux Klan.

CHAPTER EIGHTEEN

ISAAC WOKE BUT LAY quietly in the rain without blinking an eye. He had witnessed their madness throughout the night in bits and pieces, for sometimes his mind was lucid and as bright as Venus, but at other times he slid down a mountain slope into blackness—a dark, putrid pit as cold as a coal miners' burial pyre. He opened his mouth to catch the rain and slept.

At other times he meditated and entered a hallucinatory state filled with peace and tranquility. By inducing a trance, he maintained an unflinching posture, not easy with the mosquitoes and flies flitting about his head. But noting his captors' ineptitude and drunken stupor, he breathed more easily.

"The children are safe, and soon these ignorant drunks will pass out. I must survive these monstrous cockroaches a little longer, and then the light of day will frighten them away."

Isaac thought of Harry Houdini, who escaped from a steel packing case, inside which he was bound with ropes and handcuffs and thrown in the East River. Houdini had escaped in less than a minute. Then there was Geronimo, chief of the Chiricahua Apache tribe, who was able to escape General George Crook's manhunt. He dreamed of Hercules, who achieved all the feats asked of him, and still lives on, youthful and strong, among the gods.

Isaac remembered, too, the ancient African legend of the Sky God, and how mankind had distanced itself from him. Their greed, prejudice, and inability to share the world's bountiful resources had caused the Sky God pain, and he was repelled by such blasphemy. So he hid his face and distanced himself from man and moved farther away. It pained Isaac most that men had fought for millions of years over land that was meant to be shared by all.

Isaac gazed upward into the universe of countless stars, their trails becoming more luminous and distinct as they swirled around him in concentric circles. He flew on the back of an eagle and enjoyed the colorful presentation of the solar system with eyes as new as a child's. The pain in his head suddenly cleared, as did all the pains throughout his body. Smiling, he said, "Good night, my children, I can see you are safe now."

There was a short interval of nothingness, and a chasm over which he jumped, miles high—a million miles high. He said, "I wish I could tell you! I wish you could see this beauty!" He could see himself below on the forest floor, and he watched in amusement as the devils hit him again and again, finally setting his broken body aflame, not knowing that he would never feel pain again.

Isaac floated among the stars and rejoiced in the dazzling visions. He saw the glorious mountains in the west, and a multitude of mighty eagles took flight, wings reaching across the sky.

"Take me on your back and carry me away to a glorious land of peace. Fly! Fly! Fly!" He felt himself a fortunate man to leave the earth and embrace this sacred place, to fly above it all, with the fiery stars to light his way. He hoped to work his newly found magic and someday bring peace and sanity to all men on earth.

But with a piercing cry, he thought of his good mother and father, and wondered if the gods might punish him for leaving them. And he whispered, "Forgive me, my mother and father. Before I can make my home in the happy hunting grounds and make my peace with God, I must explain why I abandoned you."

At that moment a wind passed over his star and voices in the wind whispered, "You have lived with others in peace and harmony, our son;

your deeds on earth have cheered us all these many years. The spirit of God resides within you—as it does in us all—and you have never defiled that spirit. So, Godspeed, son!"

A trumpet sounded! The wind was at his back, and Isaac moved faster than the speed of light, and in a flash he reached his heavenly home.

As the shadows of the night lifted and the shifts of gray clouds merged with smoke and licks of flame above the treeline, the group hiding in the barn realized that Isaac had sacrificed himself in order to save all of them.

They dared not express aloud their dismal thoughts. Cleo seemed very ill, although her eyes were bright, and every once in a while they noticed a fleeting twitch of her lips, like a baby's first smile. They gave her water, and with the sound of each small gulp of the liquid, there was hope that Cleo might survive.

Two farmers who worked Isaac's land hitched their mules to a wagon, placed hay in the bottom, and added layers of blankets. They lifted Cleo, laid her under some quilts and covered them with burlap sacks from the barn, and tightened a tarpaulin around the outer fender of the wagon. They hoped that no one would question them, since they regularly took produce into downtown markets a few short blocks south of the hospital.

Their trip to Springhill Memorial Hospital was uneventful, although there were many cars and wagons headed north on Crowley Street, to view the fire's damage, as the smoke curled upward and could be seen from afar. Fortunately, the wagon drew no attention at all as it headed slowly south. They entered the narrow alleyway behind the hospital, as was their custom when they delivered fresh fruit, eggs, and vegetables to the hospital kitchen.

Oscar ran up the steps and returned with several of the staff members, who then rolled a gurney up to the wagon. With swift efficiency, they took Cleo quickly into the hospital's emergency room. Cleo was placed on a table protected behind white curtains, as nurses from all the various disciplines filed in. They were working frantically to save Cleo's life when Dr. Jimmy Blanchard arrived.

Together, all the physicians assessed Cleo's condition and ordered the nurses to the operating room immediately. Dr. Blanchard read Cleo's chart, assessed her condition, and immediately took control of the staff, barking orders as he examined Cleo closely from head to toe.

When Cleo had been shot, a bullet had entered her right thigh and then continued its route and was still buried inside her womb. Even though she had lost a good deal of blood, Dr. Blanchard told the tense group waiting in the corridor that he was optimistic that they could save Cleo's life.

Cordelia and Albert were beside themselves after a long night of worry. They had seen the distant smoke and fire but thought it was a forest fire, a calamity they were always afraid of with the castle buried in woods, even more so since it had become a hangout for teenagers, campers, and vagrants after it closed. That evening a number of farmers dropped by the Wallace home and told them what had happened.

The Negro community formed policing brigades, canvassed Negro residents about any unusual events, and advised families to leave their porch lights on and lock their doors and windows. Posses were appointed to check out deserted buildings in their neighborhoods. Flashlights and guns were bought and handed out by Negro storeowners to those who couldn't afford to buy them. Black farmers began cleaning their hunting rifles and keeping them ready behind locked doors at night. Farmers spirited Abe and Ruby to Savannah. No black person thought of calling the police for help, since it was well known that the city officials and fire and police departments were made up of Ku Klux Klan members.

Cordelia gathered Ophelia, Oscar, and Audrey around her that evening and had them get down on their knees to pray for Cleo and to thank God for their own deliverance from the jaws of death. When Albert came upon them in the living room, he ordered them up off their knees, complimented them for using their heads and for their good sense and skills, and cautioned them not to waste their time on pie in the sky. He continued, without another word, through the living room and up the stairs.

Cordelia sat with the children on the floor around her. "Your father distrusts religion because he comes from a long line of itinerant ministers who preached hell and damnation to their flocks all over the South but personally committed numerous atrocities on their own families and neighbors. I was just overcome with being thankful that you all hadn't met the fate of Isaac," Cordelia said tearfully. "Faith is just about all we have left. And faith in God for me is a glow that illuminates all my life."

CHAPTER NINETEEN

AGATHA CAME QUIETLY INTO the hospital room as if floating on air. Cleo heard a rustle of fabric and then her voice. Even though Agatha's lilting voice was music to Cleo's ears, a blend of African and Caribbean chords, and even though she talked for a very long time, Cleo was unable to open her eyes. Agatha held Cleo's hand as she told her tales handed down from the Asante people of Ghana. She recounted the exploits of the elusive Spiderman of African legend, who managed feats of survival beyond belief, while interweaving her own inventive endings that demonstrated the courage of women in overcoming illness, pain, and adversity. Agatha told her stories about African women and how they empowered themselves against male domination.

Cleo knew that Agatha Guilford was somewhat of a legend around the hospital, and there were rumors that in Barbados she was a sorcerer who not only held magic powers to cure people but could also destroy her enemies as well. Cleo was never afraid of her because she seemed overflowing with a sense of peace and spirituality—though she could also be firm and stubborn. While working with her at the hospital, Cleo knew better than to cross her and had made it a point to become her friend.

Agatha's stories of the brave Asante and their medical skills helped Cleo begin to accept what had happened to her and prepared her to face the future. That first night Agatha came to her bed, it was raining and Cleo was depressed because Jimmy Blanchard had just told her about her condition: he had to remove her shattered uterus for her survival, and he related to her a long story about why he had never wanted children—so thin it had struck her as false.

Cleo wept for hours after Jimmy left her room. She wept for the children she would never have, for the unconditional love of a baby, a mother's stamp on her baby—her face, her hair, her eyes. The one thing an orphan ought to be able to do is bring forth life that is undisputedly her own.

Cleo fell off to sleep and dreamed she was holding a baby, and then suddenly the baby turned into a porcelain doll that looked just like her, but it fell from her fingers, shattering. When she tried to pick up the pieces—to bring it back to life—the shards cut her, and her hands were covered with blood. She dwelled in darkness for many days and nights, overwhelmed by her loss. If it had not been for Agatha, Cleo felt she would have died.

One day Agatha came quietly into Cleo's room and said, "Today, I'm going to help you soothe that pain you've been troubled with so long."

"Do whatever you wish," Cleo mumbled sadly, "I'll never be whole again."

"Hush girl, Ol' Agatha has something good in store for you. Just lie still." Agatha turned back the covers and began to rub Cleo's arms and legs. Agatha's hands throbbed and grew warm as she continued massaging Cleo's entire body. Cleo closed her eyes. She could hear the rain falling and Agatha's voice speaking softly through the mist, her hands cool now, but beating like a heart.

"I had the 'gift' since the time I was a child. I could heal the sick, and they called on me to go to people in the old country whenever they couldn't find a doctor."

Agatha placed her cool hands on Cleo's forehead, saying, "My hand on your head brings the gift of life and health, my daughter," repeating this over and over, as if singing the repetitive chorus of a song. Then, leaving her left hand on Cleo's head, she placed her right hand on her abdomen, which was covered with bandages. Seconds later Cleo felt the pain disappear. When Cleo looked up, Agatha was holding her hands up in the air. It was then that she noticed Agatha's face was contorted, and her hands were misshapen and amazingly large and red.

After a while Agatha said, "Your pain gone out the window, now, joining the winds and blowing away." She repeated this over and over as Cleo drifted off to sleep. When Cleo awoke, Agatha was gone. And for the first time since the operation, she felt no pain—none at all.

Agatha's miracles became a favorite topic of discussion when the Wallaces and their friends came over to visit. Oscar was the only one who thought Cleo was just making it all up to entertain them and soothe her own miseries. Ophelia and Audrey rebuked him for his cynicism and said Cleo was being hypnotized. Cordelia believed it was spiritualism but never revealed to Cleo that she had always been interested in the dynamics of mysticism.

"She came to me and performed this ceremony for many days," Cleo told them, "always leaving me in some kind of trance. I would feel very drowsy, but I would hear her voice and see myself in all the scenes she described."

One day Agatha had come in and asked Cleo to roll her eyes way back in her head and then close them. "A wound needs just the right amount of blood flow, and just the right amount of air, water, heat, or coolness. Make a picture in your mind of your body, and imagine it becoming whole and healthy, and soon you will be completely healed."

After a short while, Cleo found that she could go without her pain medications. Agatha told her, "Now that your physical pain is gone, it is time to heal your spirit. Look at a spot on the wall and keep looking while I guide you. Picture a bridge that we can walk across together in comfort and peace. I will be at your side all the time, and when we reach the other side, you will be healed. Not only that, you will come to know your true self, and how to successfully clear up the conflicts in your life."

Cleo could see herself walking along a path and crossing the bridge. A swift wind pushed her along a path into a forest. Soon she came to a crossroad with signs. The sign on the right said "Freedom," and the one on the left said "Love." Suddenly a bird swooped down, hovering against the wind directly in front of her, a huge, brightly colored bird; his red, blue, and green wings fascinating to behold. It looked like a huge parrot crossed with a falcon, with long, curved talons. "*Choose!*" he crowed. Cleo thought about it for a moment and then suddenly leaped into the air, a gigantic leap as if she were performing a ballet. In the next instant she was running down the Freedom path, singing out loudly, "I choose Freedom, Freedom, Freedom!" The bird, who was hovering overhead, moved his wings as if applauding her and, in the voice amazingly like Isaac's, said, "You have chosen well, my daughter, for only after you experience freedom will you find love. And then you will have both forever." Suddenly, the bird took flight and was soon a tiny splash of color against the gray-blue horizon.

Cleo had this vision several times, and she began to feel stronger, as if she could face anything. She just had to let herself imagine the giant bird and hear Isaac's voice.

Cleo knew she had recovered before her doctors knew, and she was excited about her future. One Sunday evening, after her visitors left, she lay in her bed, her eyes shut but wide awake, considering what her options would be once she left the hospital. Somehow, her struggle to recover had physically and spiritually diminished her desire to marry. She was surprised when the thought of college instead of marriage moved to the forefront of her consciousness.

Now whenever she thought about what to do with her life, that life did not include Jimmy. She could not imagine being a doctor's wife and living a boring, meaningless life stuck in Springhill. Cleo accepted the fact that, with injuries to her pelvis and legs, she would probably never dance again, the one activity in her life that had always brought her so much happiness. She knew that by choosing "Freedom," a whole world of new possibilities would be open to her.

Cleo's dreams had changed, too. Instead of nightmares, she began to dream of wandering in bright forests, populated with beautiful, colorful plants and animals. She always came to the bridge and chose a path toward Freedom. One night Cleo dreamed she tamed the great bird and rode on its back, with a great, beautiful universe stretching out to the far horizons. She flew with fantastic speed and felt strong, healthy, and courageous.

Oscar, Ophelia, and friends who made regular visits to the hospital had not told Cleo about Isaac's fate. They had not wanted to add to her pain and suffering until they were sure she was well and on her way to recovery. But Cleo seemed to know. They were surprised when she brought up Isaac's bravery and how he saved their lives that night.

One day Cleo told them that she had seen Isaac. She said, "You know the bridge that I crossed with Agatha to the land of the Shaman? Isaac was there. He was a great eagle, an eagle with the widest wingspan one could imagine. The eagle swooped down from the sky, and I heard Isaac say clearly, 'Cleo, here's some stardust to guide you through life. It will bring you health and extraordinary luck.' And suddenly he was gone. I knew then that he was my guardian angel."

As for Jimmy, Cleo began to see him as her protector, in the sense of protecting her health, instead of as her lover. When she thought about their past relationship, those times seemed years away, like a dream she reviewed from afar and from a secure place above it all. It was like looking down on two lovers in the heat of passion but without herself, certainly not her new self, as a participant.

Jimmy was more devoted to Cleo than ever. He thoroughly enjoyed his role as knight to her wounded angel. Coming to her room daily and taking the best care of her that was possible was a joy for him. Jimmy felt Cleo was more attractive than ever, with her intellectual insights only adding to her desirability and beauty.

One day late in autumn, Jimmy knocked on her door and, getting no answer, went in and found Cleo sitting on a loveseat that overlooked the garden. She was absorbed in one of the books that Oscar had brought her. She greeted Jimmy fondly with a bright smile.

After his kiss, she patted the seat facing her, indicating that he should sit there. Jimmy was puzzled by her cool reception but took the seat facing her. He asked how she was feeling; Cleo said, "Great, Jimmy, I'm feeling better than I have in a long time. Jimmy, I want to talk to you about leaving the hospital."

Jimmy stood, pulled Cleo quickly into his arms, and said, "I can take you home tomorrow after lunch. We can order dinner from the Chicken Shack on our way to the house and have a picnic by the stream."

"Jimmy, I want to talk to you about my plans. When I leave here, I plan to go away to college. I'm going to stay with the Wallaces while I complete my application papers."

Jimmy looked at Cleo with a frown on his face and stared out the window for a moment. Then he pulled her to him and kissed her fervently.

Cleo pulled herself away from his grasp. "Jimmy, stop! Please! You never talk to me, you just overtake me, and I can't think. I want to talk with you about my plans when I leave here. Please, listen to me for a change!"

"Okay. I won't touch you. I promise. We will sit here quietly and talk about your plans." Jimmy was puzzled and surprised at these developments, but he still did not take her seriously.

Cleo turned from him and sat in the opposite chair; she leaned forward, looking at him straight in his eyes, and said, "I'm not going to live with you, Jimmy. Being here all this time has given me time to think. I want you to listen to what I have to say."

"Sure, baby, sure. What is on your mind?" He moved next to her.

"Jimmy, I've become a different person." She sighed and removed his hand from her breast and placed it in his lap. "Sometimes I think you believe I'm this naive little country girl whom you think you know. But I've become a woman. A braver woman than before."

"Of course. I respect you as a woman. I've told you that a million times." Jimmy's voice was taut; he was more than a little concerned about the direction in which their conversation was going.

"Jimmy, I will be going to Spelman in Atlanta in January.

Meanwhile, I have a great deal of studying to do in order to start as a second-year student. I want your help in making this change."

"Yes, I agree to help in any way I can. Try me. What do you want? I'll give you anything you want."

"That's just it. You'll give me! I don't want that anymore! I want to give myself something. People have given things to me all my life, from the time I was brought here. I'm tired of being taken care of. I want to see what I can do. You know—like Audrey and Ophelia. They have plans for their future. I'll be just sitting around waiting to see who will take care of me. I hate that thought! Can you understand that?"

Jimmy felt her forehead and said, "You're making no sense. I think you have a fever. Perhaps you need to go back to bed." He reached over to hold her hand, which she quickly withdrew, as she jumped to her feet.

"Let me go! I'm tired of your constant decision-making. I'm serious. I've really decided; I am absolutely determined to go to school."

Jimmy, angry now, retorted, "I see you've been hanging around Cordelia too long. But as soon as you leave here, I'm taking you to our home."

Cleo pushed Jimmy's hands away and ran quickly from him, scrambling into bed, burying her head in her pillows.

Jimmy came quickly and sat on the bed, caressing her shoulders, rubbing her back. He said, "I'm sorry. What did I do? I love you more than life itself, Cleo."

Cleo sat up and Jimmy placed a pillow behind her head. "I love you, too, Jimmy. You saved my life, and for that, I'll be eternally grateful, but I don't intend to leave this hospital and live with you again. I'm going away to school. I've got a trust fund that will pay the entire amount, and I'm going to go. I need to be by myself for a while." Her eyes stared ahead, and turning her face from him, she pronounced her intentions in the most forceful voice she could muster. "I do not want to marry you, Jimmy!"

Jimmy's face blanched with disbelief and shock. He pulled back the covers a bit and asked, "Cleo, has something happened that I don't know about?"

After a while, Cleo said softly but emphatically, "Nothing, except I want to be alone and think about my future. I am going to the Wallace home when I leave the hospital and fill out application forms, write letters, and plan what courses I need to take. I love you and thank you for everything—for all you did to save my life, for all your help. I will be forever grateful. But I know I can be somebody. It would not be right for me to not achieve something on my own."

Jimmy's look of disbelief changed to one of agitation. He was beside himself. He cast a harsh look at her as he paced back and forth around the room. It was obvious that he did not get it. He couldn't understand what caused such a drastic change in Cleo's behavior.

He walked back to her bedside, held her closely, and said, "I need to take care of you, make sure your treatment is working, make sure you are well before you leave. Perhaps we need to change your medication. I'm not going to let you leave this hospital unless I know you'll be well taken care of."

"Jimmy, I'm going to the Wallaces when I leave, and they'll take care of me very well until I go to college."

"Are you saying you no longer agree with my treatment plan?" He stood and looked down at her, defying her to continue. He stood at his full height, with his arms crossed at his chest, looking angrily down on her face, partially visible above the blanket.

Cleo was angry and frustrated, but instead of speaking, hot tears ran down her face. She had made an important career decision on her own for the first time in her life, but she still cared for Jimmy, and she was scared. He had always gotten his way from the very beginning of their relationship, and she sometimes doubted her will to leave him. Suppose she was crippled for life? Who would care for her? Agatha? Yet Agatha was the one who had devoted so many hours to her, had faith in her, and said she could be anything she wanted to be. And hadn't she, with her own eyes, seen the bird applauding her decision, and hadn't she heard the Shaman's words of wisdom?

Cleo said, "I know I'm well enough to be discharged, and I want you to assign me to another doctor tomorrow. Would you arrange that? And please close the door when you leave." Cleo turned away from him, pulling the covers over her head.

Jimmy glared down at her. Anger rang in his voice. "Okay, if that's the way you want it. Just remember it was your decision." Then he turned quickly and left the room.

That next afternoon, Oscar, Audrey, and Ophelia came to Cleo's room and brought her a large bouquet of roses in a lovely bowl, congratulating her on her recovery and decision to enroll at Spelman. Oscar and Audrey told her many wonderful things about Atlanta, the stimulating lectures of the professors, the progressive thinking of people, and other opportunities available in the city.

When Jimmy finally came to see her after several days' absence, Cleo was so startled by his appearance that at first she thought it was an apparition. He looked tired and distraught, as if he had not slept well for some time. He looked down at her with such anguish that she pushed herself up in bed, searching for answers in his eyes.

Jimmy suddenly lay down on her bed and took her into his arms. Cleo held him closely for a long time. She finally said, "Jimmy, I will love you forever. Even at the world's end, you and I will be dancing on the stars in the Milky Way to our old tunes—forever." They held each other for a long time, and she felt he understood. Cleo knew she was free to live her own life, no matter what happened.

CHAPTER TWENTY

MONTHS AFTER THE BURNING of the castle buildings and the forest fires that flared sporadically afterward, city officials had not begun an investigation into the causes. They refused to send investigators into the woods for clues as to what happened to Isaac.

But Isaac's friends knew he was gone forever. Oscar suggested a memorial service for their hero. Soon the black community grasped the idea as a way to show everyone that Isaac's heroism should never be forgotten. So they met at homes and called themselves "Guardians of Hope."

At first, they planned to hold the service for Isaac at the Clover Baptist Church, but there were bomb threats. A memorial at the springs in the forest was voted down, for Isaac's spirit transcended those blackened ruins. They planned their memorial at a secret place, at a location to be divulged only by word of mouth, without changing the flyers that had been originally distributed inviting mourners to the forest springs, where the Klan might await their appearance. They would hold the ceremony at an unexpected location.

Late that same day, several hundred Negro mourners stood before a beautiful stone on which the inscription "He Lives" had been carved; they placed it next to the gravestone of his friend, A. C. Treadwell, within the large monument that the town had built for him. They filled the walled memorial plot with flowers and medicinal plants. They made promises to celebrate each year on this date as a way to keep alive their dreams that lay smoldering in the dust.

Shortly after the devastating events that had occupied the attention of Springhill's Negro population, Albert received great news. He was offered a job in Madison, Wisconsin, at one of the largest farm research and development corporations in the country. Henry Wilson of the Department of Agriculture had recommended him. Albert had corresponded with him on several past occasions regarding the efficacy of his farm machinery inventions, and there was mutual respect between the two men. There was a flurry of preparations as Cordelia, happy as a lark, made plans for their departure. Cordelia had always known that Albert would succeed, for he had all the attributes of a leader. She was proud of him and delighted that at last their family could leave the South.

At about the same time the Wallaces were making plans to leave Springhill, Dr. Blanchard informed them he was returning to Barbados to attend to his father's business affairs. The Wallaces suspected Cleo's decision to leave him had fueled his decision to leave Springhill.

A few weeks after she left the hospital, Cleo dropped by to visit her friend, Christine Crowley. Upon leaving, she saw Jimmy sitting on the porch talking to Mr. Crowley. They were so deeply engaged in conversation that she could have kept walking down the steps without them noticing her. But she decided to go over and say a few words out of courtesy. Jimmy's back was to her, but Mr. Crowley said loudly as she walked toward them, "Hey, Cleo, it's good to see you looking so spiffy. How are you?" Both men rose, with Jimmy giving her a formal bow.

Cleo said, "Thank you, Mr. Crowley, I'm fine, and I'm thankful for having had the best doctor in the world," and touched Jimmy lightly on the arm.

Jimmy took both her hands in his and said, "Cleo, you look very well. You have a strong, courageous spirit, and I know that helped. I did want to ask for the pleasure of your company at dinner to say good-bye before I return to Barbados. You did know I was leaving, didn't you?"

"Yes, I had heard. I wish you much luck and the best of life in Barbados. And thank you for everything." Cleo turned and walked down the steps, never responding to his invitation to dinner.

It was not long afterward that Jimmy Blanchard returned to Barbados. When he arrived from the airport, his sons, who were on a school break, came forward quickly and he hugged them, surprised that they were both taller than he was. His sons took his bags and were walking toward the house when he saw Deirdre on a grassy knoll, her white, flimsy dress blowing about her hips. His wife walked slowly toward him, her hips bouncing from side to side, her chin high, smiling as if she owned the world. The sun was setting behind her, casting its spectrum of colors around her, enveloping her in its red and gold glow, causing her to look like an African princess. She began to run to him with her arms out. Jimmy lifted her to meet his kiss and held her there. He was home at last.

CHAPTER TWENTY-ONE

O SCAR, AUDREY, AND OPHELIA arrived to spend the summer school vacation organizing the library that Mrs. Redd had donated to the community. Her house, along with Isaac's collection, would become the first library for Negro boys and girls in Springhill. The young people agreed that if they put their combined support behind the project, it could be completed within a short period of time. Matthew returned from Nashville, flush with a prestigious Peabody Award to study musical composition. They decided to split the costs of food and do all the work themselves, and return to their respective schools in September.

Oscar and Ophelia walked drearily home after seeing their parents off, already feeling lonely, and together they tried to dissipate the waves of sorrow mitigated by the joy they felt with their new freedom, and their father's good fortune in securing a profitable way to leave the dismal conditions of Springhill. All the way to the Redds' home from the train depot, they talked about visiting both Chicago and Madison the following summer and applying for graduate schools there. The thought of the opportunities ahead brought them a sense of hope and exhilaration, and provided the energy they needed to plunge immediately into the work of the library. Their lingering grief over Isaac's horrible fate fueled their desire to open the library in his name as quickly as possible. Oscar had told a few people about his vision of naming Mrs. Redd's library the Isaac Naylor Library, skipping the usual "Memorial" in the title, as if clinging to a desperate hope that Isaac was alive and would one day return. Perhaps the library would be a beacon to lead him to them.

Cordelia and Albert wrote letters of encouragement to the children several times a week, praising their mature abilities and activities, and sending them money. As the summer drew to a close, they told Oscar how happy they were that he would be leaving Springhill in a matter of days and would be safely back at school in Atlanta. Oscar, however, was vexed by his mother's words of encouragement. Why were his mother's letters so filled with didactic advice and biblical quotations? How could all this drivel help him? Why had she never asked about his feelings of loss? Just because she didn't know Isaac well was no reason for her to act as if he never existed.

The truth was that Oscar was too depressed to tackle the work that lay ahead, adrift as he was in the tornado of his mind. The pain inside his head, in fact all over his body, required all his concentration to keep alien thoughts at bay, to keep him from exploding. Oscar was especially troubled that Audrey could not understand why he wanted to stay a few more weeks to finish setting up the library instead of going back to Atlanta University for his last year. Obviously, something was bothering him, and he didn't want Audrey to sacrifice her life trying to save him. He spent the ensuing weeks in a muddle of indecision and confusion.

After a week, Matthew, Emmett, and Ophelia returned to school, and Oscar knew that both Audrey and her mother, Aimee, would be disturbed when he told them he did not plan to return to school. He felt he could not face any of them right now. He was not ready to face those phony guys at school, the late night parties in the dorms, guys speaking out about things that meant nothing while the world went straight to hell. Aimee took a dim view of her daughter's urgent entreaties to persuade Oscar to return to school. She felt Audrey was endangering her own future success and was becoming too emotionally involved in Oscar's dilemma.

Finally, under duress and with earnest feelings of trepidation, Audrey agreed with her mother that they should leave, but only after a final scene when she made a last ditch effort to convince Oscar he must complete his long-held commitment to finish his thesis this year. Oscar had spent yet another day when he did no work on the library book project but instead sat through the day dejected and immobilized. Audrey approached him tenderly, as was her usual way with Oscar, but he jumped away from her as if her fingers on his arm were hot tongs.

"Oscar, I love you, but I know something is wrong. What is it? You can tell me anything! Dear, you know you can trust me!"

"I don't know, just leave me alone for once! Please!" Oscar leaped to his feet and began pacing.

"Oscar, by finishing your senior project this term, we can begin in earnest to make plans for our future, where we will live, what—"

Oscar interrupted her before she could continue, turning to her and screaming, "I will determine my future, and I, alone, will decide what to do!"

"But, darling, we have to learn to talk to each other and trust one another, don't you think? When we marry I want us to be able to discuss openly any problems that might occur."

The pain in Oscar's head was intensifying, and all he could think about was ending this conversation and being alone with his thoughts. So he said, "Audrey, it's not the woman's place to ask for the man's hand in marriage. I will ask you when the time comes, if the time comes, and I'll talk about it later, understand? *Now leave me alone!*"

Audrey began to cry and ran from the room. The next day Audrey and Aimee left on a morning train before he awakened. Oscar was relieved that the women were gone. He felt there was no one who understood him and the job he had to do. "Well," he said out loud, "if nobody else cares about Isaac's legacy, I do." He was going to make sure that people remembered Isaac, so that the sacrifices that Isaac had made were not in vain. The most important job Oscar needed to accomplish was to get the police to allow him to retrieve Isaac's books, which would become a part of the new library. In order to do so, he would have to confront the police, who had deserted the site but had not removed the yellow police tape that surrounded the giant's adobe.

After a restless night filled with dreams of war and death, Oscar visited the Springhill Police Department and asked to speak to the chief. He explained his mission and his activities thus far in his effort to create the children's library. He was surprised when the chief said that helping "Nigra" children read used books seemed like a good thing for an intelligent "boy" such as him to attempt. Oscar explained that Mr. Rufus Johnson offered his truck for the job, and it should only take a few trips.

Within a week, Oscar and Mr. Johnson, along with a farm hand named Pete—young, strong, and full of energy—began the job of removing the books. Miraculously, the inside of the adobe looked remarkably well maintained, although its facade was black with soot and there was water damage inside. Oscar shed a few tears but quickly wiped his eyes—not wanting to seem like a baby in front of the men.

After the job had been done, Oscar returned home. He ran up the steps, and looking behind fearfully, he fumbled with the keys, slamming the door shut with great force. Once inside, he repeatedly tested the double bolts. He looked in disgust at the disorder around him.

"I can no longer work in this mess!" The sight of the filthy clothes and dirty dishes, the funky smell of the rooms, the dust everywhere drove him to his bed where, exhausted, he threw himself down on his lumpy mattress, still wearing his dirty, rumpled clothes and his boots covered with mud.

His bizarre dreams flowed amidst conflicted streams of fear and loss, death and survival. He felt himself being trampled by raging horses, their hooves kicking him, their sounds deafening as they moved over him and away, leaving his body lying in the dust.

But in the next moment, Oscar was running, running, running, a train licking at his behind, its bright glare on him. And now there were people all along both sides of the track, cheering all around him, crowds of people roaring, "Run, nigger, run! Run, nigger, run!" clapping their hands in synchronized rhythm.

"No! No!" Oscar was screaming as he awakened from this nightmare, and he actually found himself lying in a grassy ditch alongside the tracks, where they used to lie in the grass as kids waiting to see passing trains. For a moment, he felt his lungs collapse. He felt like he was flat, like a paper man, with shape but no substance, as if a hot, sizzling iron had pressed him flat. "How the hell did I get out here?" His heart beat furiously and erratically. He could no longer separate his dreams from reality.

Oscar struggled through the days and the weeks. Most days he paced back and forth through the house, casting harried looks at the stacks of books in piles all around him, as well as those in the library, waiting for classification.

One quiet Sunday morning, he sat at his desk and wrote a letter of apology to Cleo for causing her injuries and ruining her life. "Most of all, though, I need to speak with Isaac. I would like to hear his voice, and listen to his words. I must ask his forgiveness. If it had not been for me, Isaac would still be with us today."

One evening Oscar took to the streets, clutching his saxophone case close to his chest. His saxophone was safely wrapped in its protective silk cloth inside its case, which he stroked as if it were made of fancy leather instead of coarse, worn plastic. He walked jauntily down to the railroad tracks. He continued alongside the sprawling power plant and soon found himself out past the mansions on the far side of Springhill. He strolled at a leisurely pace across the beautiful grounds of the white cemetery, its grass so brilliantly green that even at dusk it caused him to wonder if heaven could ever surpass its luminescence. At last he arrived at the place he had known was his destination, the walled mausoleum where A. C. Treadwell was buried.

Oscar sat on the low wall where a profusion of flowers formed a beautiful, many-hued bed, the place where they had made a memorial for Isaac only a short time ago, yet it seemed to Oscar as if centuries had passed. He sat on the wall near the jagged stone, carved with the words "He Lives" barely visible above the blossoms piled in exuberant profusion around it, the last blooms of the summer past.

He placed the saxophone strap over his shoulders and, lifting the horn skyward, trilled a scale in honor of the sky's purple streaks and the white clouds running, like a herd of fleeing cattle. Oscar played a master suite of his own creation. Later, a rimmed moon came up over the hills, a sign of rain, but Oscar didn't care about that, and so he continued to play on into the night, paying no attention to the encroaching fog that rose from the moist earth like a gauze-cloaked woman searching for her lost children; bending, rising, falling over one grave and then another. Oscar could almost hear her crying in a high voice—a whimper in the wind. Suddenly, Oscar's attention was drawn to another voice, and there was something about its tone, timbre, and cadence—quite firm yet compassionate—that made Oscar instantly decide to do whatever it commanded him to do. But this new voice made no demands of him but said softly, like a fog horn heard in the distance, "Why you out heah, boy, in the dead of night, makin' all this heah ruckus?"

Oscar whirled around, searching the mist, and gradually saw a face as black as night emerging from the curtain of gray. "Sorry, sir, I thought this was the last place anyone would be disturbed." He walked closer and said in a too cheerful, startlingly unfamiliar voice, "I'm Oscar Wallace. I, I—live on the other side of town."

"I know who you are, Oscar, and I'se acquainted wid where you live."

Oscar stood his ground, but his heart was pounding; he asked, "Have I met you? Who are you?"

"I'se the grave-digger and ground-keeper, and we lives right over there," he said, turning around and pointing his fingers somewhere into the gray mist.

Oscar moved a step closer and said, "Who? We? You have a family?"

But the old man ignored the question and came forward, grasping

Oscar by the shoulder. Oscar felt his bony fingers on his back, almost like a claw, and thought, *Am I completely crazy, or am I dead?*

The old man said, "Sit down heah, boy! I jus' come by to find out who wuz so upset out heah to make sad songs all night long. What's the matter with ya, boy? Somethin' trublin' ya?" His soft voice was like molasses, viscous and smooth.

Oscar hesitated, while allowing the old man to lead him to a place on the wall, a wall he could only feel, now that the blackness of the night had deepened. Oscar looked skyward, trying not to look at the man's face, and noticed the moon had disappeared. Instantly, he lost his bearings and thought himself in some kind of floating abyss, as if he were supported in the air by the clouds and fog. Just then, the man's grasp moved him downward onto the hard seat and kept him grounded there. The wall was wet from the fog, smooth and slippery, as though many had sat on it before him, gradually wearing down the edges.

Oscar wanted to run, but he knew in the fog, there was nothing to guide him this dark night.

Oscar heard the man's voice in the mist begin its wobbly tone, as if it came from underwater, "Ya got troubles, ain't ya?"

"I'm terribly confused and I'm troubled. There is no one I can turn to. I'm lost. I'm sick and I feel terrible." The words, in a still unfamiliar voice, had tumbled off his tongue, unexpectedly. Without any forewarning, Oscar began to cry, the sobs coming from deep inside, as though a dull knife were coursing through his body, exorcising all the painful pieces inside. He was an open drain that now joined this sea of floating mist. He looked up but could not determine where his tears ended and the fog began.

Oscar tried to control himself as the voice said quietly, slowly, droning with a bassoon's timbre and rhythm, "Listen, I'se gwine tell you somethin'. Dis heah graveyard full of people, most of them want to live longer to keep on doin' devilment. Mos' peoples worry 'bout dyin'. But dar wuz 'em who never give death a thought. Dey wuz too busy, day in, an' day out, jes' livin'.

"My ole Mammy, she ain't buried out heah, and she ain't in no other decent earthly place, neither. She walk fifty mile a day on dat plantation near heah, carryin' wood on her back, totin' cotton on her back, white chill'ens on her back, anything else dey made her carry, and I cried to see her back. They wuz marks all 'cross her back lak a jigsaw puzzle. She ain't never complain. Jus' keep going. She knowed if she do dat, they's a better day a'comin' for youngans who wuz comin' after her."

Oscar had stopped crying, lulled by the gravedigger's slow and heartfelt narrative.

The old man continued, "But take some of these new Negroes, they complain 'bout dis and dat. Well, it ain't fair to family that gone before to complain. Some of them, tossed in a ditch when they passed on, or burnt alive wit no bones to bury, jes lik Isaac."

At Isaac's name, Oscar jerked and looked at the man but couldn't make out his face in the dark and fog.

"He wuz a good man, a good man. You think he done what he done jus' for you, boy? 'Twas for all of us. Listen to what I say, boy. I lived long enuf to speak the truf. Member what your forbears been through. Your ancestors' brave blood still flow in your veins. Good blood! You heah? 'Cause they kept on, kept on, kept on, walkin' down that long road, so your path be shorter'n theirs was. Your walk ain't nothin' compare to theirs."

The old man's voice wound through the darkness, like a long road through a treacherous forest, winding steadily upward toward a sliver of light.

When Oscar opened his eyes, the sunlight was pulsing through the clouds as he lay on the stone wall with one arm flung over his face. Then, he saw "He Lives" directly in front of him. He shuddered and jumped to his feet. There was no sign of the gravedigger, and a part of his consciousness wanted to believe he had been dreaming. Yet, he remembered everything, all the words, all the stories, and the sound of the old man's voice trailing off into the fog.

After his visit to Isaac's memorial and his encounter with the gravedigger, Oscar began to play his saxophone daily, marveling at the sweet, spontaneous sounds that became complicated harmonies, the scales growing into mini-symphonies. He played the blues, he played jazz, and he played classical. His body and mind became whole and peaceful again.

Within a few weeks, Oscar wrote a proposal and sent the finished product to his professors in Atlanta. His thesis would document the lives of rural farmers, their hopes and fears, their stories of survival, their dreams for the future of their children. Positive responses came quickly from all the professors involved, and Oscar embarked on his research.

CHAPTER TWENTY-TWO

CLEO'S DRAMA PROFESSOR, DR. Roscoe Pembroke, was introducing her to Douglas Davison, the eminent director of Broadway shows and a renowned playwright. Davison had walked into the cafeteria with Dr. Pembroke as Cleo was exiting, a few steps from the door.

"This is one of our outstanding drama students, Miss Cleo Marshall. Miss Marshall, Mr. Davison. Mr. Davison is seeking a talented lead for our new play, a musical adaptation of *Cleopatra*, and I had just the moment before recommended you. By the way, you two have something in common. Miss Marshall comes to us from Springhill, Georgia."

Douglas said, "I was born in Valdosta, Georgia, but I don't think I've ever heard of Springhill. I've been living in New York for the past fourteen years, so I may have forgotten about some of our beautiful Georgia towns."

"It's tiny, not many people have heard of it," Cleo said. Her interest was piqued when she heard he had lived in New York. Cleo felt the tingle of a blush rise in her face. Mr. Davison was looking into her eyes with such directness (or, she wondered, was it intimacy?) that she felt a bit startled as his tall body leaned forward to make eye contact with her. Cleo said, "I'm pleased to meet you, Mr. Davison. I thought of applying to Barnard in New York, but I decided Spelman was the best school for me."

"Call me Doug. I'm not a professor, so everyone calls me Doug. And I'm delighted to meet you, Cleo."

Cleo immediately brought up her friendship with Gwendolyn Redd, who was touring in Europe with Katherine Dunham after the successful opening of her latest show in New York. "I'm hoping to visit her on Long Island when she returns."

Dr. Pembroke broke their locked eye contact by announcing that he needed to get to his next class. "I'll leave you two to make plans for the audition. Cleo has a great deal of talent in both voice and drama."

When Dr. Pembroke was gone, Doug pulled out a chair at a nearby table and asked, "Could you take a moment to tell me about yourself?"

"Sure. I have no classes for the rest of the day and was just going to the library to study. I can do that later."

He sat next to Cleo, and she loved his smell, a clean, masculine scent that was all male perfection, bottled, but taking nothing away, yet adding the outdoor air to its aura.

Doug looked deep into her eyes again with his brilliant large commanding ones, set deeply in his dark, angular face, with an exquisitely prominent nose and cheekbones.

Cleo thought, *He's too dramatic, and he takes up too much space. But, of course, that's what he does—he's an actor.*

"Cleo, Dr. Pembroke mentioned that you have a background in voice and drama. I've auditioned a few students and was just telling Roscoe—Dr. Pembroke—that I'm not quite satisfied with the candidates for the lead."

Doug explained his need for someone with dramatic stage presence, a strong singing voice, and a graceful bearing, although he didn't expect a freshman student to be a seasoned actress—yet. He began to tell her the story of the musical.

Cleo interrupted, saying she had studied Shakespearian tragedies when she attended Springhill Normal School.

Doug's interest was obvious. "Oh, you're not a freshman, then. Good!"

Cleo wondered how much she should tell him about herself and decided he did not need to know everything. So, she said, "I took some advanced courses at Springhill Normal, and after passing basic first-year tests here, Spelman allowed me to take sophomore courses."

"Somehow, you seem more mature than the average student. I'm having trouble trying to relate to these very—what can I say—young, inexperienced girls and boys. It takes some getting used to."

Cleo hesitated a moment but then admitted to him that she was older because she had suffered an accident and was in a hospital recuperating for several months. Then she added, "You may have read about it in the papers. I was visiting a friend's home, singing, believe it or not, when a Ku Klux Klan gang surrounded the house." Then Cleo added, looking down and shaking her head, "I really don't like to talk about it."

He seemed to move closer, although there was no perceptible change in distance between them, as he continued looking into her eyes and said softly, his voice compassionate and understanding, "Thankfully, you recovered. So, what are your goals in studying here, Cleo?"

Cleo loved the sound of her name coming so deep from inside his larynx and caressing his lips like a song. "I want to be an actress some day, maybe even a writer. So, I am studying English, drama, and theatre. And the basic curriculum, of course. But I've been in many song and dance recitals."

"Ah, one of us. Have you done much acting?"

"When I was younger, I acted in pageants, things like that. I sang, recited poetry. It was all very amateurish. I studied ballet for years, but I no longer dance."

"The lead needs only to sing and act. And I have already noticed that you move and walk like a dancer. That's very important for the stage. When would you be free to audition?"

Cleo said, "Now. I have a few hours free right now!"

Doug looked at Cleo with admiring eyes and smiled. "Cleo, I like your spontaneity. I can tell we are going to get along very well, no matter how you do at this audition. Let's go!"

Somehow, Doug made Cleo feel comfortable, and she had no nervous apprehension at all. She was thrilled to be given this opportunity in the middle of the school year, her first weeks away at school. She thought, *Just wait until I go home tonight and tell Audrey and Aimee!* Cleo followed Doug across the campus to the Theatre Department, like a frisky puppy dog follows her master.

By the end of the day, Doug knew he had found his star. Cleo joined the cast as the lead in *Anthony and Cleopatra*. Rehearsals started the next week.

As Cleo walked off the campus and down the hill toward the Durant home at 190 Boulevard Street, she felt her life was now exciting and full of promise. She was inspired by the talented director and got along well with her three leading men. Christopher Long, a dashing, tall football star, played Caesar. Maxwell, a humorous, rambunctious young man, played Mark Anthony, and Fred, a slim, energetic youngster, acted the part of Ptolemy. The cast hung together and met each other in the cafeteria for meals. Cleo was very fond of her companions, and they became a popular group that attracted others to their circle. The whole project was a mammoth production, requiring a large chorus and armies, larger than any production the Drama Department had ever undertaken. Doug's direction displayed his genius. Cleo noticed that he was always focused, replete with energy and ideas, and commandeered every aspect of the production, including the music. She loved every rehearsal, every song, the camaraderie of the cast and the director. Most of all she knew she had mastered the role of Cleopatra; she became Cleopatra (*What a coincidence*, she thought), and she had her body, her mind, her vitality, and her soul.

For a long time, she had thought Doug was just a dreamer. But occasionally she would see mail on his desk from New York and from famous people—even a famous Hollywood director—and eventually she became aware of the esteem with which he was held by renowned theatre people throughout the country. He aspired to bring plays to children in elementary schools and to have productions in the parks around the city, as was done during Shakespeare's time.

Cleo loved to listen while Doug talked about theatre. It was an education in itself—listening for hours to his plans, watching him draw the diagrams for sets, hearing him describe the places he had mounted festivals—Scotland, England, and Canada. His goal was to establish a repertory theatre for Negro actors and bring plays to the masses. He named many distinguished persons who were involved in this movement, and she recognized many names: Ossie Davis, Ruby Dee, Paul Robeson, and Canada Lee.

When the production of *Anthony and Cleopatra* came to an end, with rave reviews in the *Atlanta Daily World*, as well as the major white newspaper, the *Atlanta Constitution*, Cleo became a star of sorts—and not just on campus. The newspapers had singled her out as someone headed for an "illustrious career on the national horizon," as the *Atlanta Constitution* put it. The next few days were exciting and productive, with a flurry of congratulatory telephone calls and invitations to parties and dinners. For the first time in her life, Cleo was surrounded by classmates near her own age, and she began to feel like a real college student at last. She and her friends met for study as well as play. She had become a valued member of a very exciting group of students— arts, theatre, music students—men and women whose company she enjoyed.

When Doug left for New York at Easter, he did not say good-bye or write a card with a personal message. Cleo began to suspect he was married and had a family. She missed him terribly, and a feeling of longing for his presence came out of nowhere, occasionally bringing unexpected tears of sadness to her eyes.

Cleo knew that Doug was her teacher and director. He had never suggested anything more. Yet, she felt he cared about her in a unique way that contributed to her sense of self-respect. He never seemed interested in her personally, yet he singled her out all the time—came to her table in the cafeteria if she was alone, and talked with her for hours about the theatre. He took long walks with her across the campus, never inquiring about her past or her personal life, but seemed delighted in talking to her about his theatrical ambitions.

Cleo thought this was all she wanted from their relationship—until he went away. Now, she had to make a dedicated effort to put Doug out of her mind. She decided to forget him and spend more time with her new friends. She had obviously been naive and foolish to think that she and Doug had some special bond.

Cleo lay sprawled on the green grass, watching other students weaving their way along the curving paths. Spring had come to Atlanta; the campus felt as if it were newly reborn. More students than she had imagined in residence appeared out in the open in full force. It seemed that the girls of Spelman College and the boys of Morehouse College were welcoming springtime, the warmer weather having driven them from their small, airless dormitory rooms. They looked so different from the young people in Springhill—more sophisticated, worldly, and obviously much richer, judging from the clothes they wore. Cleo was soon joined by her friends, and they engaged in horseplay and lounging on the green lawn—soft and springy, like carpets woven with flowering threads of colorful flowers. Most were her theatre cohorts, along with their groupies—art, music, and literature students. They were picnicking on snacks and engaged in parodying fictional characters. Cleo held a somewhat vaulted place among the other actors, perhaps because of her obvious friendship with the renowned director, as he was a magnet that drew other students to him.

Cleo was sitting on the grass leaning against Christopher, the very handsome football player who had been her Caesar in *Cleopatra*. They were playfully teasing each other, his arms around her shoulders.

From out of nowhere, she heard Doug's voice say, "Cleo, let's go inside where we can get a drink of coffee and talk."

Cleo looked up in surprise, for she had not seen him approaching, nor had she known he was back from his trip. She excused herself and got up to follow him, but not before she noticed the cynical raised eyebrow on Christopher's face.

After getting coffee in the common room, Doug led her to his office, a small room with bare walls on which ladders were leaning, and he pulled two wooden folding chairs over toward the one window. The sun was bright, the rays filtering through several dirty streaks that ran vertically down the entire length of the long window.

They sat silently for a moment, sipping coffee. Cleo had always felt important because Doug had taken her into his confidence and asked her questions about situations that had come up in the play, and even what she thought of specific cast members. She had actually known him to activate some of her ideas.

Today, however, she sensed something different. Doug was looking at her in an unusual way. It was odd that he had asked her to accompany him here after coming upon her and Christopher kidding playfully with each other on the grass. Was that it? He was jealous, and he just wanted to cut it off, show his power, command her presence: "Come with me to my casbah."

Cleo thought of how he had left, not a word of interest or a good-bye. She felt suddenly angry at the men of the world who didn't give a damn about a girl's feelings. She held her head down, afraid to look him in the eye, for fear that he would read her thoughts with his intense eyes.

Doug began telling her about the conference he had attended in New York, but his words were flying past her, missing her receptive capabilities, as her mind raced with questions: *Can I trust him? Is he married? What is his life really like?*

Finally, she could make out his words. He was telling her what he was trying to accomplish. A different kind of theatre—a repertory theatre—and he wanted her to be a part of this plan. Sometime in the near future, perhaps as soon as next year, after his year in residence was over, he hoped to organize a troupe; set it up in New Orleans, Atlanta, or some other colorful southern city; and eventually take plays on tour throughout the country. Cleo relaxed, and her excitement soared. *He wants me to join his troupe!*

He continued, saying that New York had lost its sense of purpose after its short-lived renaissance, and that presenting realistic plays with theatrical flair, accompanied by the sounds of the South—the fields, homes, music, lingo, and voices—was the way of getting average audiences to love the theatre. He would present the folkways of his people with such interest that Negroes all over the country would embrace art, theatre, music, and dance. His productions would be fluid and creative; they would include black artifacts and soulful music. That is why he decided to return South and travel about, listening to the voices of the people instead of following the old theatre model of redoing white plays with black characters and calling it "Black Theatre."

Later, when he walked her home, Cleo invited him inside. They sat in the kitchen with Aimee and Audrey, eating pie and drinking coffee. When he said good night to Cleo outside under the light of a full moon, he looked down at her, squeezed her hand, and walked in long strides back up the hill.

For weeks, Doug talked to Cleo about his work, but after a time she realized he had said nothing about his life. But for her it was enough to become his soul mate, to share the theatre. Many nights they sat in the kitchen at the Durant home or in his small office with the dirty windows. Cleo loved being in his presence, with his energy spiraling down on her like invisible electrical discharges in the air. He would erupt with passion every once in a while as he spoke, which often propelled him off his chair. He paced around the room, waving his arms to make a point, before sitting again facing her. Cleo understood him! Believed in his passion! They talked of writing plays together; original, authentic plays of the Negro experience. Cleo was at a loss to express the intense passion she felt for his dreams of the theatre—it was almost as if they were of one mind.

Doug and Cleo were walking across the campus one evening when she finally asked him what his childhood was like. He was talking about the value of southern roots and she asked about his home in Valdosta. He took a photo out his wallet and said, "This is a picture of my little girl. Her name is Jasmine. She's seven years old, and she still lives there."

Cleo was shocked because she had snooped around and found out he was not married, and she had never seen him with other women, outside of working relationships. "Who does Jasmine live with?"

"She lives with my Great-Aunt Millie and her husband, Peter. They are old, but energetic and lively."

"Does she ever come to live with you?"

"The last time I saw her, she was two years old." Doug and Cleo were sitting on a stone bench, looking toward a fountain, the lamps inside the library casting a dim ray of light on them through the windows.

Cleo felt as if a stake had been driven through her heart. She scrambled up and started walking away quickly.

Doug caught up with her and grabbed her shoulders, turning her around to face him. "What's the matter? Did I offend you?"

"You have that gorgeous daughter, that beautiful girl; how could you do such a thing to her? How could you? What kind of man are you? How could you just walk off and leave her with other people?"

Doug tried to hold on to her, but Cleo pulled herself away from him. She ran across the soft grass, almost tripping and falling as the tears obscured her vision. When he came upon her at last, she was standing at Auburn Street, waiting for the light to change. He came up behind her and held her to him. "Please don't do this. Talk to me. Don't run away, please."

Cleo was crying hysterically. "I trusted you! I put you way up there somewhere on a pedestal only to find out you're a child deserter—the lowest of the low. I never want to see you again!" She ran across the street against the light, but no cars were coming. She walked, lost and forlorn, until she was exhausted. Finally, she hailed a cab to take her home.

When she reached the house, Audrey was sitting in the living room reading a book. Seeing Cleo's red, teary face, Audrey rose slowly, baffled, and then rushed to her. She asked, "What happened, Cleo?" She was holding her at arm's length, looking her up and down. "Did someone attack you, Cleo?"

Cleo fell in a lump on the couch while Audrey went to the bar and poured a glass of sherry for both of them. "Just sip this for a few minutes and relax, and then you can tell me all about it."

After Audrey heard Cleo's story, she held her and soothed her and told her that she definitely understood how she felt, especially since Jasmine was the same age now as Cleo had been when she had been brought to the castle.

Cleo finally said, "Just when I'm happy, demanding nothing, and love my theatre courses and my director, I discover he is an abominable person!"

As she cried, Audrey hugged her and whispered, "Have you ever told Douglas about your childhood? That you are an orphan?"

"But don't you see, Audrey? He has never asked me anything about myself. Doesn't that tell you how disinterested he is in me and my past?" She began crying again. "He's such a goddamned egotist! And I have been thinking he was God all these months. I never want to see him again. Never!"

Audrey said gently, "Never say never, Cleo."

Cleo avoided Doug's usual haunts on campus and worked at home for the next few days.

She and Audrey talked more frequently, and Cleo was happy to hear that Audrey and her mother were going to Cambridge in June for a few days. Carl Ellis, Audrey's fiancé, was graduating from Harvard Business School. They planned a wedding in the fall, and he would then become the CEO of the Durant Insurance firm in Atlanta.

Audrey suggested, "While we're gone, invite Douglas over, cook him a meal, and talk out with him what you are feeling and why. You know you adore Douglas, so don't give up on him so easily. When Oscar came to see me after his breakdown, we spent hours discussing how we felt. We agreed we would be friends for life, but not lovers anymore. And we remain great friends. You do the same. Don't end it without giving it a try!"

Cleo returned to the campus only when the drama department scheduled an important meeting. Dr. Pembroke gave notice that students who expected to take part in any productions the next term must attend. Cleo volunteered to work backstage with production instead of acting, in order to learn all the skills required in theatre. At least, that is what she told her professors. Actually, she was attempting to distance herself from Doug.

One day Doug came into the little room backstage where she was working on production schedules; he stood quietly beside her. Cleo knew he was there without looking, but she did not speak and he did not touch her.

Finally Cleo turned to him and, seeing the pain in his eyes, held out her arms, and he reached out and pulled her to him. She could feel his heart beating loudly, a match for hers. He kissed her passionately, but she pulled away from him, her eyes demanding answers.

Doug opened up to Cleo at last and told her Jasmine's story. "I was thirty years old and had never married. When I met Jasmine's mother, Bessie, I was working as a part-time actor and going to graduate school, and she was a singer, working on the nightclub circuit. We were not friends, just casual lovers, but I fooled around with her on several occasions. When she told me she was pregnant, I didn't believe it, even though we had unprotected sex. I offered to pay for her to have an abortion, and she took the money."

Cleo listened, barely breathing, as Doug went on, "I hadn't heard from her for almost a year when she phoned to say she was going to Europe on a long gig, her chance of a lifetime, and she wanted me to keep the baby until she returned. I told her that was insane, and I wasn't going to do it. I had paid for an abortion she agreed to have, and I had not heard from her since. I had heard nothing about the birth of the baby, and I didn't know anything about babies. Besides, I was going to be in an off-Broadway play within a few weeks.

"However, she came to my apartment building one night in a cab; she must have known I was going to be home that evening, because she handed the baby to my roommate, Earl, telling him that I was expecting her, and left immediately. For a few days, I tried to get in touch with her, but there was no answer. I called my mother and brought the baby to Valdosta. She took care of Jasmine for two years, and after my mother died, my great-aunt and great-uncle kept the baby. I supported Jasmine by sending money, but that was my only connection or contact with her. The only feeling I had about this child was a deep-seated anger that I had been completely tricked and was paying the price. There was a good possibility that the child was not even mine."

Cleo could barely look at him. Though he was obviously baring his soul, she could only see his story through the prism of her own pain. Could she ever love a man who'd abandoned his child? Who would have, if he'd had his way, aborted her? At that moment she realized that if she were to truly love Doug, she would have to be instrumental in reuniting him with his daughter.

At first, Doug could not understand Cleo's intense reaction to his abandonment of his child. Actually, under the circumstances, he had thought he had done the right thing. This new point of view forced upon him by Cleo, a person he held in very high esteem, was an unexpected surprise to him. He had figured her to be one of those rich, beautiful southern belles, who had always gotten everything on a silver platter. He understood that women reacted differently from men regarding their responsibility to nurture children. Yet, Cleo's heartfelt interest in the child caused Doug's heart to expand; he realized he was in love with her, a woman with a soft and warm heart for others. The next morning they made plans to go together to Valdosta and bring Jasmine to Atlanta for a visit with them. He would rent an apartment off campus.

As they drove to Valdosta, about two hundred miles south, Cleo told Doug about her life as an orphan. He listened intently; at one point, he parked the car to hold her, as they both kissed each other's tears. They arrived in Valdosta, planning to spend a week with Doug's Great-Aunt Millie and his Great-Uncle Peter, both in their late eighties. The house had a musty smell, mixed with the scent of cooking—perhaps collards and ham hocks. Cleo and Doug had already eaten and had brought with them ham and cheese sandwiches. Aunt Millie and Uncle Peter declined the food, offering their own soup instead.

Doug had told Cleo that the last time he saw them, they were well and apparently healthy, but obviously that was no longer true. They were stunned by the older couple's appearance, and asked them over and over about the state of their health, but neither of them seemed to follow a thought for longer than a few seconds. Doug commented to Cleo that they had aged considerably since he last saw them five years ago. Their voices were weak and watery, like sounds bubbling up from a shallow pond.

Cleo went immediately to Jasmine, who was sitting on a small chair and staring into the fire when they arrived. She did not move to greet them but gave them half-smiles, turning her face to avoid eye contact with them. No matter how much Cleo attempted to excite her with the books, games, and dolls they brought for her, Jasmine was unresponsive. Cleo decided finally to back off and give her time; she left the homecoming to Doug.

The house was one of those old southern-style planked homes, with a wide porch under a slanting roof and four posts that appeared too fragile to hold it up. The house was rough-hewn and had obviously seen better days, but the floors had been recently swept clean. One could smell a lemon oil scent that must have been used to dust the table in the center of the room, on which they dined. Cleo found an album on the table and began looking at the pictures, and soon Peter and Millie came to the table and began pointing out the people in the pictures and explaining their relationships. Gradually they became more animated. Soon, Jasmine joined the circle and began pointing out and naming the people she knew in the photographs.

Jasmine had the face of her father, with high cheekbones and a wide nose, but instead of his intense eyes, she had large soft brown eyes that glanced shyly toward her father as if he were a complete stranger. Doug spent some time trying to get her to remember his last visit, without success, and there were no pictures of him in this album. It was obvious, however, that the elder couple had taken care of the child, for she was clean and smelled of soap, and her hair was neatly braided in cornrows. And the more they conversed with Jasmine, the more animated and intelligent she appeared.

Both of the old people spoke in trembling voices, obsessing with their fears about what would happen to Jasmine after they were gone.

They said they were considering putting Jasmine in an orphan's home nearby and asked Cleo and Doug to accompany them the next morning to look at the place. When Doug explained that he wished to take Jasmine back with him, they said they wanted her to stay close by, so they could still visit one another, and they knew the good people who ran the home.

The next morning, they ate a hearty breakfast, including biscuits that Millie had made, but the old people begged off from taking the trip, telling Doug repeatedly that he should remember where the orphanage was. "Pass the fire station about ten miles out on the main highway, you'll see it—just keep on going left after the corn fields. It's the Masonic Hall Orphanage."

It was while they were driving through a rainstorm toward the orphanage, lost and confused even after asking directions, that Cleo had a panic attack. She had been trying to read a road map when the rain began pouring down, and she suddenly found herself shaking uncontrollably. She told Doug that her chest hurt and hung her head out the window gulping for air, but torrents of rain soon washed into the car. Doug pulled Cleo back inside and tried to hold onto her shaking body. He reached in the back seat for a blanket and put it around her, but she still trembled convulsively and gasped for air. Cleo screamed, "Help me! Where are we going? Save me, I'm drowning!"

Doug pulled the car over to the side of the road, which from his vantage point seemed to have vanished altogether in the flood that now descended from the black sky. He pulled Cleo to him, felt her heart, and noticed her erratic heartbeat and the sweat covering her body. Doug reached over into the ice chest that he always traveled with and took out some ice and a thermos of water. He rubbed ice on Cleo's wrists, forehead, and arms, and directed her to "breathe with me now, in and out." He repeated this over and over, his breathing rhythms showing her the way. Doug was thankful for his experience teaching actors relaxation exercises before going on stage.

Within a few minutes, Cleo was breathing normally again, but she looked pale and weak. Doug decided to wait out the storm, so he bedded Cleo down on the back seat while he kept an eye on her. As soon as the rain subsided, Doug abandoned the plan to look for the orphans' home and turned onto a road likely to have lodgings so that Cleo could rest.

Doug pulled up to a roadhouse along the country road, thankful that there were signs of life; in fact, there were signs up for just about everything: gas, food, liquor, music, and rooms. A number of Negro men were leaving as they drove in. They opened the screen door and entered a dimly lit bar and restaurant. They took a booth near the center and ordered a cola for Cleo and coffee. Doug spoke to the clerk about taking a room immediately, saying that his wife was ill. The man spoke in a crude backwoods dialect, barely understandable, but seemed to be saying that there was one, although they would have to share a bath. Sight unseen, Doug agreed to the inflated price, because torrents of rain pounded down again, making thunderous sounds on the tin roof. After drinking their beverages, they went up to the little room, with its streaked windows and sagging beds, and both fell asleep in spite of the loud music that occasionally competed with the thunder for their attention.

Later in the night, as the storm's intensity increased, a crack of thunder caused Cleo to cry out. Doug leaped from his bed and rushed to Cleo, putting his arms around her. "What is it?" he asked. "Don't be afraid." Cleo sat up in bed, staring wide-eyed into the shadows, as if the dream she was having refused to release her from its grip. But it was not a dream, nor was it a prescient vision. Cleo had entered the dark days of her childhood that her rational mind had attempted to protect from her consciousness all these years. Douglas gently rubbed her back, whispering, "Cleo … Cleo, where are you?"

She was in the castle's living room. The walls were alive with dancing figures thrown by the leaping fireplace flames. Cleo was looking up into a man's handsome and familiar face. A. C. Treadwell, the castle's benefactor, whose portrait atop the fiery-eyed steed had once made her tremble with fear, was vivid and alive above her. And she was not afraid. She was leaning against his knee, wearing yellow pajamas with little brown baby bears on them, looking back and forth dreamily between Treadwell and a dark-skinned woman with wild coal black hair and grey eyes, who Cleo knew at once was her mother. Cleo's mother was laughing, white teeth glinting in the firelight. As Treadwell talked he rubbed Cleo's stomach back and forth, making her feel safe and warm. His leather pants smelled like horses—and as she breathed in, she was becoming drowsy.

All at once the door banged open and the wind rushed in along with a dark, wiry man with muddy boots, Papa Solomon. He fell to the floor and everyone stood up. Solomon looked at Cleo's mother with bloodshot eyes, saying, "Come on, woman, we leavin' this place."

And then Cleo was swept up in Treadwell's arms, and he was rushing out through the hall door, telling her to run up the stairwell and to do it quietly; "Don't make a sound." He smiled and winked, but she could see fear in his eyes. Cleo sat quietly in the stairwell on a high-up step. She could hear Papa Solomon shouting her mother's name: "Hester! You my woman! You coming wit me! That devil Treadwell can keep his half-breed child, but you and me is leavin' this house for good!"

"Solomon, you drunk again." Hester was pleading with him, "Go to bed and sleep it off. I ain't goin' nowhere wit you."

"Don' play me for a fool, you lying, cat-eyed bitch! I can prove it! Ya layin' with him on that cot out in the barn, ya hair and his is all over it! I seen it! And I ain't standin' for it no more!"

Cleo could hear screaming and shouting, the sounds jumbled in her ears. She put her hands over her ears to block the noise, but a strange moaning continued, like an animal in pain, which she realized was coming from herself.

Her mother was screaming, "I ain't goin' nowhere wit you, you good-for-nothing drunk! I hate the sight of you!"

A door slammed, footsteps were running. Hester came in and pulled Cleo to her feet, whispering urgently, "Rebecca, come out the back way, quick!"

Then they were outside running downhill, very fast. Cleo could hear Treadwell's voice behind them saying, "Stop it, Solomon. Put down that gun."

Solomon was shouting, "Treadwell, damn you! I'll kill you, you wife-robber! You dirty, lowdown scoundrel!"

Hester wrapped her skirt around Cleo. Behind them, the shouting came closer as the two men ran down the hill toward the river.

Hester picked Cleo up and waded into the water. She laid Cleo at the bottom of a little canoe and covered her with branches.

She walked deeper into the water pulling the canoe. Cleo could hear her mother crying and see her terrified eyes through the branches as she pulled the little canoe out into the stream.

There was a loud sound, like a crack of thunder. Cleo pulled the branches back and looked through the leaves, but where her mother had been wading, there was only black water. She was alone in the canoe, rocking back and forth, and Solomon was standing on the banks of the creek, pointing a gun at her. Another shot rang out, but it was Solomon who fell. Then Treadwell was walking into the water and taking her into his arms.

Treadwell carried her for what seemed like a very long time, her body trembling against him. He brought her to a little gingerbread house, where for a time an old woman looked after her, but even as the acute shock of what had happened finally began to release her from its grip, a terrible sickness took hold of her, and she couldn't get out of bed for a very long time. Dreams and waking were indistinguishable, each filled with nightmare images and frightening sounds, like a gramophone played at the wrong speed. When she finally emerged from the fever and delirium, she was back in the castle again, and she was called Cleo.

Cleo looked at Doug, clearer than she'd ever been.

"My name is Rebecca! Rebecca is my name. I didn't know it until now."

Tears streamed down her cheeks, and she sobbed into his broad shoulder. But her buried grief was tempered with relief. She finally had a context for her life, a past that, however painful, would allow her to more confidently embrace the future.

Even during their breakfast of pancakes and good strong coffee at the Sunrise Café, Cleo continued to tell Doug about her life: the beginning, the middle, and with some prodding, her romance with Jimmy.

Doug told Cleo that he had never known his father, and that his own mother had left him with relatives and moved somewhere far away. Like a patchwork quilt, they stitched their past lives into a whole piece, sharing also their hopes for the future.

When they returned to Millie and Pete's home, they set about relocating the old couple to a safe housing complex just around the corner from their former dilapidated home.

They wanted to remain in the same neighborhood where they had lived for so many years, and now they were just across the street from the red brick Baptist church where they worshiped each Sunday. They invited the preacher over for dinner one Sunday afternoon, and even though it wasn't quite the same as a wedding, the minister watched as Cleo and Doug swore on the Bible that they would make the union whole by marrying in a church of God for the child's sake.

Cleo and Doug had already decided to take Jasmine with them when they returned to Atlanta. They were very excited about the possibility of using Cleo's early life story as a theatrical drama.

Jasmine was thrilled that she was going to Atlanta with her daddy and Cleo. And with her as a family member, Cleo and Doug talked through the night about the kind of relationship that would nurture their child and provide her with all the advantages she deserved.

Cleo and Doug were married in a beautiful ceremony in the chapel at Spelman College with Jasmine, Audrey and Carl, and Aimee Durant in attendance. Jasmine smiled and kissed everyone, dancing around and holding out her skirt as if to curtsy, saying over and over, "I feel just like a princess in my new clothes."

Cleo, Doug, and Jasmine went to New Orleans for their honeymoon, staying in a two-room suite on the top floor of a house owned by Aimee Durant's aunt, close to Jackson Square.

The story of Cleo's early years and the tragedy of her childhood became the hit musical drama, *River Full of Tears*.

CHAPTER TWENTY-THREE

THE ISAAC NAYLOR LIBRARY finally opened to the public with great fanfare, its celebration covered by the leading Negro press as well as the white press. There was a picture in the newspapers of the mayor shaking Oscar's hand. But the enlightened Negroes of Springhill took the mayor's promises of monetary contributions to the library with a grain of salt and continued their successful efforts to maintain a large volunteer staff.

Even though his parents pleaded with him to move to Chicago, where all the family had now settled, Oscar refused to leave Springhill. He taught philosophy and literature at the new Wallace High School, located on Isaac Naylor Boulevard, where his flamboyant manner and brilliantly dramatic discourses took hold of a new generation of eager students. Oscar also taught the brass contingent of the band, and whenever the neighborhood youngsters heard those melodic saxophone tones coming from an empty bandstand on moonlit nights, they would join him; they would either play together or listen to him play solo. The music that had kept him sane in times of trouble was a balm that the teacher, writer, and leader now passed on to young people. Oscar was the publisher of a community newsletter, the *Springhill Reporter*, and he also served on the boards of the hospital and the Negro Improvement

League. And like his father before him, he never entered a church unless there was some special program for the good of the community.

Oscar traveled to Chicago once a year to visit the family. He was especially proud of his little sister, Ophelia, who was working on her Ph.D. at Chicago University. A devotee of Carl Rogers, she hoped to put his client-centered therapy into practice on Chicago's South Side.

Occasionally, Oscar visited Emmett in Harlem, where he learned the ins and outs of journalism in order to expand his own small town newsletter. When he visited New York, he often stayed with Gwendolyn and Richard Lewis in their Harlem mansion. Gwen was involved in dance choreography and had roles in a number of popular musicals.

Cleo and Doug's musical drama, *River Full of Tears,* was being performed in colleges and small theatres all over the South with plans for an off-Broadway tryout.

Oscar's honorary prize, to be presented to him at Atlanta University's graduation ceremony, became the event around which Cordelia Wallace planned the reunion of their entire extended family. Cordelia wrote letters to everyone and badgered them with weekly cards requesting their presence.

In June 1941 Albert and Cordelia Wallace traveled to Atlanta for the reunion. Cordelia was thrilled that everyone she invited actually came, with the exception of Douglas, whose theater company was in dress rehearsals in New Orleans. Mrs. Redd came by plane from New York with Gwen, Richard, and baby Michael. Oscar was being honored for his writings about his civic work among the tenant farmers and other disenfranchised poor people in the South. He had published numerous articles of his interviews with tenant farmers. During his years of interviewing the poor, Oscar wrote and published their stories in his small but powerful Springhill newspaper, which had reached an interested audience of ardent reformers all along the eastern seaboard.

Emmett ran a series of Oscar's stories in New York's *Uptown News,* and they had attracted a large audience. Oscar's book featured a collection of common folk's voices, which reflect their heartfelt emotions. Oscar compared their voices to the plaintive sounds and phrases of music and poetry. His work was popular among scholars, writers, and artists of all races. His book, *Climbing Parnassus: Poetry, Folklore, and Music of Southern Negroes,* was an instant success. Oscar had taken astonishing photographs of his subjects, their expressions honest and sincere; each person appeared to reach out and touch all who saw them. Oscar developed all the photographs himself in his basement laboratory.

During the graduation ceremonies, the renowned teacher, race leader, and author, Dr. W. E. B. Du Bois, presented Oscar's award honoring his creative genius. Abe Swartz made a few brief remarks honoring his former student, having been given a specific time limit because everyone was aware of his customary loquaciousness.

Cordelia was proud of Oscar but still worried about him. It was no secret among her children and a great number of her friends that Cordelia wanted Oscar to leave the South, and she hoped his new success would provide this opportunity. She was worried for his safety, and she habitually contacted professionals in high places as soon as she became acquainted with them for news of job openings for her "educated and accomplished son, the distinguished author, musician, and community leader."

The throngs of celebrants climbed the steps to the magnificent buildings of Atlanta University; its facades gleaming like ancient polished stones in the brilliance of a perfect summer morning. The attendees teemed with anticipation and with a sense of heightened purpose, looking outward with the shining and proud eyes of those who are certain they have accomplished a great deal in spite of the odds set against them. As people bustled about—the women in elegant spring dresses, men in white or light colored summer suits, graduates in blue, gold, and black—it was easy to see that this cheerful atmosphere would prevail, at least until the celebration was over.

As Cordelia and Albert took in the colorful scene, the gorgeous summer day's breeze wafting softly over them and they were reminded of those times in the past when college campuses figured so prominently in their own lives.

Then they saw Oscar, wearing horn-rimmed glasses now, looking a bit nervous and uneasy. He stopped short of reaching them, for he was joining Audrey and Carl. They watched in wonder as Audrey and Oscar embraced, and Carl rose and put his arm around the shoulder of his wife's former lover. What great friends all of these young people had become, a new, more liberal, and forgiving generation.

Oscar turned and walked toward them, and both parents felt a great surge of pride in the kind of man he had become. One could almost hear those golden apples dropping from the tree, its roots thundering deep into the fertile earth, the fruit scattering their seeds everywhere. Even though he needed to get back to the podium, Oscar spent a long time with his parents, kissing and hugging them as if he hadn't just talked with them.

Carl and Audrey hosted a party in Oscar's honor. The celebration took place in their new Durant Insurance Company offices, which had once been the home of a white insurance company. The building was big and lavish, its old and ornate wainscoting reverent with age, the chandeliers gleaming. At the end of the evening, groupings of family and friends offered toasts for success, friendship, family, and blessings for the future.

"Bravos" and applause resounded, and the conversations were filled with that enthusiastic energy that one experiences when the excitement of the moment garnishes hope and ideas for the future, and like fog dispersing in shafts of sunlight, creates an aura of grand expectations.

Cordelia was especially gratified, for she had pulled this whole celebration off without any idea of how really great her reunion would become, and now she looked about with pride and satisfaction. She was especially delighted that Jasmine would be staying with them for a few days, while Cleo joined Douglas in New Orleans. Albert turned to Cordelia and said, "You did it, my darling!" He bent over and kissed her.

The festivities had put Cleo in a pensive mood, and after congratulating Oscar wholeheartedly, Cleo moved away from the others and sat at a window off the great hall. *So, here we all are,* she mused.

161

Feelings of hope and aspiration overflowed the room tonight, as if we were in the presence of a future—glorious, true, and clear. This was an evening burnished with a glow of gold dust that seemed to brush off on everyone. But magic is enchantment and life is reality, and the music always ends. If I'd been asked to speak, I would have talked about the strife of life, which was far from the minds of most. We've learned to abandon the truth in search of pleasures inspired by golden moments such as these, where intrusions of reality are not welcome.

Now that I am a writer, I often wonder if words will conquer my suffering. How do I get to the truth about life without drowning in that dark water again? If it hadn't been for Treadwell, I wouldn't have been born. How different would my life have been if I had known he was my father? He provided for me but never acknowledged me. He saved my life, but his so-called rescue brought me more pain than one could ever imagine. No one wants to hear about all the pain we cause each other through our injustice, our prejudice, and our wars. Only Oscar and Emmett spoke of the impending war. And only a few of us clapped at their remarks. Why dampen everyone's spirit?

The celebrants were leaving in small groups, as the lights in the building dimmed. Cleo joined them, as they walked outside in the dusk of a beautiful evening. Some looked up, admiring the beauty of the night sky, its perfection and symmetry. Cleo could hear their murmuring voices of hope rising into the dark night. Those voices helped to lift her spirits, but only for a moment. Once they turned the corner, they would plunge into darkness, and have only the fireflies and the white azaleas to light their path down the hill.